THE SPIDER:
THE SERPENT OF DESTRUCTION

MASTER OF MEN!

THE SERPENT OF DESTRUCTION

By Grant Stockbridge

ALTUS PRESS • 2019

CHAPTER 1
SERPENT OF BLOOD

R AM SINGH crouched, his hands cupped between spring-steel knees. His dark eyes glinted beneath the down-sweeping edge of his turban.

"Ready, *sahib*," he whispered.

The Spider took two swift strides forward, stepped upon the cupped hands. Ram Singh tossed upward, and his black-masked master, cloak swirling, seized the bottom rung of a fire-escape ladder. With the smooth precision of an acrobat, he went up hand over hand until his feet found purchase.

He merged with the night, a dark, moving shadow amid blackness. Windows were open and curtains fluttered their ends in the warm May evening, shuttling from yellow light into darkness. Radios crooned or squawked jazz. People talked above the racket, noisy and care-free. They little suspected that the Spider crept soundlessly past their windows, that across the roofs of the city strode another gaunt shadow, a giant whose fleshless jaws grinned horribly, whose glittering sharp scythe was poised, awaiting the Spider's command—the shadow of the specter of Death!

The shadow that was the Spider crept on until it reached the fifth floor and there paused beside a window. Within the apart-ment, a girl sobbed, a strangled horrible sob that had nothing to do with tears.

Wentworth's two shots were lightning
swift but deliberately aimed.

The Spider peered in. The girl was on the floor. An amber robe trailed as she pulled herself on stiffened arms, legs dragging, across the floor. Her hair was amber, too. Its smooth flow hid her face. And her breath was sobbing. Upon the back of her amber robe was a sprawling pattern of crimson… of blood! The hilt of a knife formed the center of the pattern. It had been driven up to the guard in her back!

The Spider flung inside, dropped to a knee beside the girl.

The death-weary head did not sway toward him. She dragged onward, her breath horrible in her throat.

"Alice," he cried sharply. "Alice Cashew! Who did it?"

The girl crawled on, but the gasping of her breath became a word sound. "Blood!" She panted. "Bloody!" Two fearful rasping coughs tore her—"Bloody Serpent!"

The Spider caught her beneath the arms, lifted her so her eyes were glassy upon his.

"Quickly," he urged. "Was it the Big Mick? Harrigan? Tell me why."

3

THE SPIDER

The staring eyes focused vaguely. A gleam shone there for an instant. *"D-do—"* Once more a racking cough. *"Dope!"* It was a scream.

The specter of Death stepped into the room. The girl collapsed across the Spider's arm. He did not see Death's jaws gape in laughter, did not see the specter, fondling his blade, crouch in a corner to wait....

Dope and the Bloody Serpent.... The Spider's thoughts raced. He had come this girl, Alice Cashes, seeking information about Big Mick Harrigan who had thrown her out after they had long been lovers. He knew Harrigan's liquor racket had been killed by repeal and he had thought to learn to what rascality the gang would turn its vicious strength. He had believed that Alice might talk about Harrigan through spite. But murder had stalked before him and, though she had talked, it had been a Sybillic utterance. Dope and the Bloody Serpent. He frowned beneath his mask.

Carefully, he eased the girl's body to the floor, then with quick, practiced hands began a search of the apartment. The bureau first attracted his attention. He crossed to it, an alert, quick-moving figure of a man, nearly six feet tall, his face hidden by a black, skirted mask, a soft black hat on his head. Even the heel-length cape could not hide the powerful figure, the vital strength of his athletic body as with hands and mind he sought the answer to Alice Cashew's dying riddle.

Her very death told him he had struck a warm trail. Once again the keen mind of the Spider, mysterious avenger, nemesis of all who defied the law, had flashed ahead of the dragging logic of the police. He had seen that the gangs must turn to some new racket that would offer the same enormous income, the same opportunities for graft and corruption that liquor had supplied.... He finished with the bureau, found a trunk beneath the studio couch and knelt beside it.... Seeking the gang's new racket, he had found a dying girl who screamed of dope.

The Spider straightened from beside the trunk. Nothing there. He thrust it back beneath the couch, turned toward a tawdry, worn davenport—and in mid-stride stiffened into immobility, listening. From outside the window, he caught a high, piercing whistle. It was Ram Singh's signal of warning!

THE SPIDER darted to the apartment door. He flicked aside the cover of a peephole in its middle, snapped it instantly back into place. Three men and a woman stood out there, and there was a key in the hand of the foremost man. The Spider's swift fingers snapped home a bolt. Through the door a voice snarled:

"Open up! We've got you surrounded!"

Beneath the skirt of his mask, the Spider's mouth opened in soundless laughter, but there was grimness about his eyes. The battle he loved was on, the battle for Justice which he ceaselessly fought. And he found the enemy worthy. They moved swiftly, seemed even to know his moves in advance. For they had murdered a girl he sought to question and now they had moved swiftly to trap him. It indicated a powerful and efficient organization.

The thoughts were as a lightning flash. Even as they flicked across his mind, he acted. He stepped to a phone in the hall, clear of possible shots through the door. His right hand turned a pistol's black mouth toward the fire escape window, ready if they attacked there.

"Police!" he spoke rapidly, as if telephoning, but the receiver rested untouched upon its stand. "In a hurry, please." He waited a moment. "Police? Rush help to apartment 5G," and he gave the address. "Rush help! Rush!"

He strode to the window, and a bullet sang upward from the black depths a bullet whose gun was silent. The lead dug into the ceiling. The Spider slipped back to the door, twitched aside the peephole cover. Lead smashed through the glass. The gunman was not in sight, but a door ten yards down the hall was open a crack. Surrounded? Yes, but the gangsters had been driven to cover for the moment. They would wait for police to smoke out their quarry and the Spider had gained time.

Lips tightened into a fighting smile, he returned alertly to his search of the apartment. As he worked, he hummed a light aria in a pleasant baritone. His tones were happy. Behind him, in a corner, the invisible specter of Death straightened, smiling.

But if the Spider knew Death was behind him, he paid no heed. His sensitive, strong fingers massaged a cushion. He slit it with a knife, and a handful of folded packets of white paper fell to the floor. He opened one, found it full of crystalline white powder. He touched a flake to his tongue, nodded soberly. Cocaine....

There came a sound at the door, and the Spider darted to it, black cape flying. His hand slid beneath his left arm to a compact kit strapped there, extracted a file-like piece of metal. It had teeth set at an angle, all slanting the same way. He jammed that into the crack of the door. Let them try to force it now! He whirled to the phone, once more demanded the police in excited, frightened tones, and this time he actually put through the call.

He spun back to the apartment, ducked into the bath. He hung the cape in a closet and revealed—not the suave, quiet clothing that was typical of him, but a flashy wide-striped suit with a pinch back coat, high-waisted trousers with gaudy suspenders. The black hat followed the cape to the closet. The flat automatic and the mask went to the kit beneath his arm. The mask's removal revealed the Spider's keen, vital face, a face not six persons in the world knew wore the mask of the Spider, the face of Richard Wentworth, wealthy young clubman, sportsman extraordinary, secret soldier of dark warfare with the forces of the underworld!

IT WAS the face of a strong man. The gray-blue eyes were those of an idealist, of a man who could dedicate his life to the service of humanity. And there was a reckless gayety there, in the quirky, tilted brows, the love of adventure that would permit a man to smile while gangsters intent upon his death snarled at the door, while a woman lay murdered and police sped in their swift radio patrol cars toward him while Death sharpened its scythe in the next room.

But even as Wentworth smiled at his reflection in the mirror, his hands were busy. Putty from the makeup pack that was part of the kit beneath his arm thickened the bridge of his sensitive, intelligent nose, raised it into a beak. Water smoothed his black, curly hair into a patent-leather cap. A touch of caustic tilted

7

his outer eye corners upward, and he rouged with so deft a touch that he acquired the natural, rosy cheeks of a high-blooded man. He lightened the healthy tan of his lean jaws. With a cigarette stuck between drooping lips Wentworth nodded to himself. The disguise was complete. He was a lad-about town, a flashy youth on the make.

Three strides took him to the pitiful body upon the floor of the next room. The cord from the girl's robe went quickly beneath her arms and with a deft jerk, he had lifted and carried her to the bath. He raised the window, eased the body out and tied the cord to an awning brace. Sirens were wailing now in the street. He had a minute, perhaps two. He closed the window, spun into the next room.

On an ash tray he built a small fire of cigarettes. The decks of cocaine, he flushed into the sewers. Then he looked swiftly about. A blood stain on the rug! He covered it with a carelessly tossed magazine, then dropped into a lounge chair beside the cigarette ash tray, began to grind out the smoking butts. There were a dozen there, a tray filled with ashes. Smoke had stratified the room. Another cigarette dangled from his lip. He laid his coat across a chair so that his flashy gold and black suspenders showed, draped a leg across the chair arm—and picked up a magazine from the table.

Thirty seconds later, the bell rang peremptorily. Wentworth got up slowly, yawning, and slouched to the door. Twice more the bell rang.

"Wait a minute, can'tcha?" Wentworth said impatiently, his words slightly accented, his voice thinner than natural. A trick manipulation and the wedge slid free and into that neatly concealed kit beneath his arm. He twitched aside the peephole cover, let out a gasp of amazement and stared at the two policemen outside.

"Come on, open up!" one growled.

Wentworth fumbled with the door latches.

"Sure, sure!" he gulped. "Right away!"

He got the door unfastened, reeled back as it was slammed against him. The two police pounded in. One darted on into the apartment; one shoved a gun against Wentworth's ribs.

"Now, what the hell's goin' on, here?" he demanded. His brogue was thick.

THE COP was hefty, with broad shoulders and a beefy face. Wentworth in his slouch-shouldered, hollow-chested pose seemed no match for him. He allowed himself to be hustled back into the apartment.

"Nothing. Nothing's the matter," he gulped. "Who said there was?"

He let himself be shoved into the chair where he had been sitting. The cop who had rushed ahead turned a dark, snarling face.

"We got a call to come here," he said. "Somebody yelled for help."

"Geez!" said Wentworth. His mouth hung open.

The cop stood in front of him with a gun hanging in his hand. He thrust his sharp face at Wentworth.

"What you doin' here? This is a woman's apartment."

Wentworth ducked his head quickly. "Yeah, my girl friend

lives here. Alice Cashew. She was out when I come in and I sits down to wait. I'm reading and smoking" he looked toward the ash tray and the magazine on the table, and the cop's eyes followed. "Then you ring the bell, and…."

Wentworth's hands jerked up, palms outward as he shrugged. "Honest, that's all I know. Ain't nobody called for help here."

Exasperation twisted the dark cop's face.

The beefy policeman took off his cap and scratched short, red hair. His finger nails made a noise. "S'pose we call headquarters," he mumbled. "Must of got the signals twisted."

Wentworth got up and put on his coat, pulled a cap out of the pocket. "I don't like this," he mumbled. "I'm goin' out when you do."

The other officer turned his dark, sharp-nosed face about, looking around the room. He shrugged, started for the door. And at that moment a woman's scream rang out into the night—a woman screaming in horrid fright in the darkness outside.

The two cops and Wentworth spun toward the window.

"Watch this guy," the sharp-faced man snapped. He plunged to the window and stared out. He looked down, up, then to each side. He cursed, spun about and headed for the bathroom door. He reached it in two bounds. Wentworth watched him, open-mouthed. Stupidity was written large on his face. But well he knew what had happened. The gangsters had struck: again!

A gunman on guard below had spotted the girl's body swinging out the window, had guessed at Wentworth's trick and the woman with them had screamed to give warning, to betray him into the hands of the police! He half-turned toward the hall as if to stare at the second cop. The man's gun ground into his ribs.

"Don't be after trying any funny business," the officer growled. He was frowning, his blue, small eyes alert.

In the bathroom, the other cop was cursing and grunting. He staggered into sight and laid the girl's body on the floor. He straightened, glaring at Wentworth.

"Oh, no," he jeered, "you ain't done nothing at all, nothing at all. You just murdered your girl friend that's all!"

The cop's gun ground harder against Wentworth's ribs. Death, in his corner, laughed.

CHAPTER 2
THE SERPENT OF GLASS

WENTWORTH STARED at the body of the girl and forced his eyes wide. He shook his head slowly from side to side, ignored the sneering prods of the police and moved, heavy-footed, toward the dead girl, arms hanging.

"Alice!" he said hoarsely. "Alice!"

The sharp-faced cop watched him with bright, suspicious eyes. The other called sharply, "Hold on there."

Wentworth walked on. He stood over the girl, then dropped down on his knees. They jarred dully. His whole body slumped.

"Oh, Geez, Alice!" he moaned.

He did not touch the girl, only crouched miserably above her and moaned. He began to sway, to gabble out word sounds.

The sounds became ordered. He threw back his head, eyes shut, and intoned in what seemed to be Yiddish, a lament.

"Shut up!" ordered the dark cop.

Wentworth wailed on, his voice shrill.

"Shut up!" the cop snapped. He twisted his fingers in Wentworth's hair, yanked him to his feet and thrust him stumbling backward against the chair. He sat down hard. The Irish policeman stood with gun hanging.

The sharp-faced officer spun toward the hall and the phone. But before he took two strides, the lights winked out.

"Hold him, Pat!" he rasped.

Wentworth went out of the chair and down on his knees. He seized the Irish cop and swung him into the seat, ducked aside as the other man slapped heavy feet toward him. Wentworth circled and pounded toward the door of the apartment, hitting the floor heavily.

"Come back here!" he roared, in his best brogue. "Halt, or I'll fire."

"You damned fool, Pat," the dark cop roared out behind. "I've got him here in the chair."

Wentworth snatched open the door, found darkness in the hall, too. He slipped out, clapped the door shut. But he did not run blindly from the building. His next move had been calculated, even as his escape had been arranged when he shouted in Hindustani to his servant, Ram Singh, while apparently he was bewailing the girl's death in Yiddish. He ran only ten yards, to the door from which a gangster had fired on him!

As he reached it, he snatched a lock pick from the kit beneath his arm. A swift moment's work and he darted in, flinging to one side to dodge possible attack.

"Save me!" he gasped. "The cops!"

The white beam of a flashlight blinded him. He raised his arms. Outside he heard the police pound by, shouting, heard their feet beat down the stairs. It would take them minutes to learn that he had not fled the building, other minutes to get help to surround and search the apartments.

"The cops!" he panted again.

"Quiet, fool!" a man snarled. "Keep the light on him, Tess."

Footsteps came lightly toward him. The man with a hat brim dragged down across his eyes, a white silk muffler concealing the lower half of his face, loomed in the edge of the light.

The Spider's mind was racing. He had hoped these gangsters would still be here, for through them he hoped to trace the mysteries of Alice Cashew's dying cry of *Dope* and *Bloody Serpent*.

HE WAS calm as the practiced hands of the man in the white muffler searched him. The compact tool kit beneath his arm was built into a padded hollow in his clothing so that it seemed a part of his hard body. Yes, Wentworth was calm. He could not know that the specter of Death was even now crouched in this room, crooning over his sharpened, ready scythe.

The crooning of Death was silent, but there was a dull, murmuring voice in the darkness that was as mournful as death.

"You can't do this to me," its monotone stated. "You can't do this to me."

Wentworth's eyes narrowed. Who could that be? Swiftly, he

13

made his face blank as the man with the white muffler finished his hurried search and stepped in front of him again.

"Now what's this all about?" the man demanded.

Wentworth spoke rapidly, with a furtive glance at the door that any second might resound with the blows of invading police. "I'm on the prowl in this place, see?" he said. "I seen one of youse take a shot at that door down the hall and decides this ain't no place to prowl. I starts out, and the super of the building comes in downstairs and I got to hide till he's gone. He hangs around, but when he goes and I try to get out I runs into some cops. They're working me over when the lights go out and I beats it—here."

The man's eyes glinted. "You came to the wrong place. Get out."

Wentworth cringed before his glare. "O.K., pal," he whined. "I'll get out, but youse'll be sorry. I can get youse out of here."

The man's hand darted forward, and Wentworth saw a ring glint redly as it seized his coat lapels, jammed him back against the wall.

There was a revolver with a long-barreled silencer in his other hand. It gouged into Wentworth's belly.

"Get out!"

Wentworth cried out as if in fright. "I'll show youse how to get out!" he said frantically.

The eye of the flashlight began to move toward Wentworth, then abruptly the ceiling light flickered on and Wentworth saw the occupants of the room. Two gangsters with drawn guns, a girl in red with the flashlight that still dazzled Wentworth's

14

eyes, and behind them, on a studio couch, a dark girl in blue who lay sprawled out, asleep with her mouth open.

The room was outfitted sparsely in the manner of furnished apartments: varnished table and chairs, a davenport violent with reds and greens. On it sat a fat man with hanging hands, a man Wentworth knew. This was the source of that mutter in the darkness, the mutter that had said, "You can't do this to me." The fat man repeated the phrase again now, without hope.

Wentworth's eyes darkened. The man was Nino Carlotti, who ran a fine restaurant. It had been a toney speakeasy but his usually smooth black hair hung awry over eyes that were dull and feverish. His fat cheeks sagged, "You can't do this to me," he said again—hopelessly.

WENTWORTH'S EYES jerked back to the girl in red. She put out the flashlight and continued her slow saunter toward him. Her silken dress was tight enough to show the movements of her hips. She seemed absurdly young until she came quite close; then Wentworth could see the hard lines about her mouth corners. The brows had been plucked to a high thin line that made her gaze seem wide and innocent. The eyes were hard as blue china.

"He's talking sense," she drawled. "Better listen to him, big boy."

The man with the white muffler jerked up his gun and slashed at Wentworth. The blow was quick as the strike of a rattlesnake, but Wentworth was ready. He fell away from it. The gun hurt and made him dizzy, but he was far from out. He lay still on his face on the floor.

"That was a smart trick, big boy," drawled the girl, a sneer in her voice. "Maybe you wanna get caught…."

The smart crack of a slap cut her short. The girl's sharp heels stumbled backward. She strangled on a curse.

"When I want your advice, Tess, my dear," came the soft voice of the man in the muffler, "I'll request it."

"Listen, big boy," the girl said sullenly, "if you think you can knock me around—"

"Quiet, Tess!"

"—you got another thing coming. I ain't no Alice Cashew that you can stick a knife in and you can't frame me like you're going to frame this other dame."

"Will—you—shut—up?"

"Go spit in your hat," Tess told him tartly. "Stand still! One more step and so help me gawd I'll empty this gat into your belly. This ain't Washington, and I'll be damned if you're going to knock me around."

Washington! Wentworth caught at the word. Then the operations of this gang extended beyond New York. How far reaching were its ramifications? Wentworth recalled certain facts that newspaper clippings had revealed. Services that scanned the newspapers of the world snipped all items about crime, collated them and delivered them to Wentworth. What Wentworth remembered suddenly was that dope addiction had shown a steadily rising percentage for several months.

Petty crime had increased enormously; robberies and kidnappings had become more numerous, and arrests and convictions less frequent. Was it possible that he had stumbled on part of a well organized, nation-wide movement? Were the old alcohol racketeers turning to dope and other major crime as the dying woman's hint had indicated?

Such high pressure methods as racketeers used, if applied to narcotics, would mean hundreds and thousands of the country's youth turned into addicts, primed for crime and immorality, headed for prisons and hospitals and death! It meant the Bloody Serpent would worm into the homes of the middle class and poison them, would turn sturdy working men into….

"Listen," whined one of the gangsters. "Let's fight this out some other time. Me, I want to get out of here. If this bozo knows a way out, let's wake him up and find out. You can bump him soon as we get clear."

"Yeah," growled the other, "that goes for me, too."

A way out? Yes, Wentworth knew one, but it was not for these gangsters to take. The Spider knew now what he had risked death here to learn; knew that the gang had wide, perhaps national, ramifications and that it was turning to the narcotics racket. He would know where to strike next, could easily find Harrigan, the gangster lover of the murdered girl. But it was time now for the Spider to go. At any moment, the police might return.

Abruptly, Wentworth recalled that other girl on the couch. He realized she must be the one these crooks planned to frame for murder! Wentworth's lips twitched. If this girl was to be framed for murder, she must be snatched from the grasp of this gang.

To Wentworth's ears came again the mutter of Nino Carlotti. "You can't do this to me." It was without emphasis, without any hope. "You can't do this to me," over and over in the same tone.

The Spider's eyes hardened. He could not carry Carlotti to safety also, but tomorrow, he vowed, he would learn the meaning of that strange, futile phrase....

WENTWORTH STIRRED, groaned and flopped over on his back, his right hand falling on his breast. He felt the sharp prod of a shoe and looked up into the down-thrust face of the blonde in red. She kicked him again, a sweet smile on her mouth.

"Stir your stumps, bozo," she ordered, "and lead us out of here." Her gun was in her hand, but not pointed at him.

Wentworth blinked up at her stupidly, took in the rest of the room while he threw a convulsive arm over his eyes. The other two men were watching the girl in red. The leader was peering out into the night through a slit of the drawn shade. His left hand was outlined against the dark green and Wentworth saw that on the first finger of the left hand there was a spiral ring of scarlet that caught the light and glinted, a spiral that formed a serpent.

The Bloody Serpent! Wentworth dropped his arm, looked back to the girl. Still the gun was not pointed down at him.

Wentworth swung both his legs to the left, against the girl's ankles, knocked her feet out from under her. She plunged down across him with a small smothered scream, hands out-thrust. Wentworth snatched her gun, rolled clear.

The two gangsters stared, open-mouthed. As the Spider

lunged up on one knee, they snapped out of their surprise. Two hands darted for weapons. Death, rearing up in his corner, laughed.

Wentworth's two shots were lightning swift, but deliberately aimed. The first gangster leaned weakly back against the wall. The mouth of the other gaped foolishly. A bullet hole between his eyes was like a third, bloodshot orb.

Before the two slumped to the floor, Wentworth leaped to his feet. He flicked a glance at the gang girl. She lay motionless, knocked out by the fall. Even as he saw this, Wentworth sprang aside. The leader's muted gun coughed its lead harmlessly into the wall.

Wentworth squeezed the trigger again, held the dull click of the firing pin as it struck an empty chamber. He dodged aside again, feeling the hot fan of lead past his cheek, and hurled the useless gun squarely at the muffled face of the leader.

The man ducked, spoiling his third shot; and before he could again point his unwieldy, long-barreled weapon, Wentworth was upon him. His fists thudded home, left and right, shoulders rocking. The man slammed against the wall, went down and out. His left hand struck the steam radiator beneath the window. The spiral serpent ring shattered, became a spatter of glittering crimson fragments on the floor. A serpent of glass.

Wentworth frowned, muttered a single exclamation of dismay. He had wanted that ring. It must be some sort of insignia of identification between the gangs. It would have been useful. Too late now. Muffled, excited shouts heralded the police, summoned by the Spider's two swift death shots.

19

He stooped and snatched aside the white muffler, jerked off the concealing hat. A mass of wiry white hair jutted up like a cockatoo's crest. The man was heavy, but meticulously dressed. His jaws were full and florid, the nose slightly bulbous. There was something familiar about the face. Wentworth's brows contracted in thought.

The shuddering impact of shoulders ramming the door jerked him from his study. He whirled toward the dark girl in blue still sprawled upon the couch, sleeping with her mouth open. A squint at her eye pupils told him she was doped as he had suspected. No chance to wake her. Yet to leave her in the apartment would involve her with the police. And the gang talk had indicated that she was innocent.

Another thump of shoulders against the door. It was steel, built to withstand fire and sneak thieves, as in all modern apartments. But even steel could not long withstand that assault. Wentworth moved silently across the floor, jabbed his tool of saw-tooth steel between metal door and wooden frame, raced back to the girl's side. His hand flew again to the kit beneath his arm, snaked out a length of cord not much thicker than a match stick. It seemed fragile as spider web. And such indeed it had been called—the Web of the Spider. Wentworth's lips twisted in their old mocking grin as he padded the silken cord and tied it swiftly beneath the girl's arms. Fragile that silk might seem, but it tested to seven hundred pounds!

He caught up the girl's limp body with an ease that bespoke the trained strength of those wide shoulders, and strode to the window, turning off the lights on the way. Another blow shuddered the door. It creaked and a screw popped from a hinge with a miniature explosion. Wentworth calmly lowered the girl out the window, taking a turn of the thin cord about the steam radiator.

When she dangled opposite a dark window two stories down, he snubbed the cord and tied it in a knot* which his practiced jerk from below could loose. Then a reckless smile on his lips, he spun back toward the two who lay dead upon the floor.

His hand slipped a cigarette lighter from his pocket and he pressed its base to the foreheads of the two who were dead. In the darkness, the result was invisible, but Death, cleaning his crimsoned blade, must have spread his fleshless jaws in laughter. For Wentworth left upon the foreheads of the two men his own calling card of Death, a tiny crimson spot with hairy, sprawling legs—*the seal of the Spider!*

---

* AUTHOR'S NOTE: There are several knots which can be untied from afar, but the one Wentworth used was a modified form of the sheepshank knot which every Boy Scout will instantly recognize. It is tied by doubling the rope so that three strands lie side by side, then taking a half hitch around each end of the doubled portion. This is the sheepshank. Wentworth's modification was that he severed the central strand of the triply doubled portion. As long as there was strain on the rope, the two half hitches held tightly on the portions of the rope that bridged the portion he had severed. When the weight was relaxed, these half hitches became loosened and an efficient shake on the rope, then a sharp jerk brought the Spider's Web back to him—leaving, of course, a small portion fastened securely above. Once those hitches bite into the rope, they will hold until the

It took but an instant, then he looped another length of the silk about the radiator and threw the loose ends out. The dangling line twisted about arm and leg to lower him slowly, he swung out the window, lowered the sash to within a fraction of an inch of the bottom and let himself downward into black space.

WENTWORTH MOVED as rapidly as he dared. Had he carried enough of the silk, he could have dropped both himself and the girl to the blackness of the rear areaway below, made a silent retreat over fences to another street. But, compact as was the kit beneath his arm, he could not carry great lengths of even so fine a rope.

He reached the sill two stories below, where the girl dangled. A swift thrust with a jimmy of chrome steel from that same

weight which draws them taut is eased. A jerk of course, an arresting of the weight, then a renewed strain, would tug it loose. For that reason, Wentworth used this method only in extremity—as when he lowered Grace Puystan, unconscious, from the window. Ordinarily, for himself, he simply looped the rope about a chimney, or some similar object, threw the loose ends over and descended gripping both cords. When he wished to draw in the cord, he released one end and pulled on the other.

Personally I have tried the trick with small success, but that was because I did not have the marvelously flexible cord which the Spider used. Silk, as all my readers will know, comes untied more readily than any other substance and it is necessary to have a cord that will relax of itself when weight no longer strains it tight. This silk accomplishes by its marvelous elasticity.

kit, and the catch of the window was pushed back. Within a small dog yapped. Wentworth raised the sash, climbed in. The dog snapped at his ankles. Wentworth's mouth tightened. If there was any one in the apartment…. A man's voice pierced the darkness.

"Who is that?"

Wentworth snarled out, "Keep quiet, you! Or I'll shoot!"

He dragged the girl in, whipped loose the telltale silk cord and ducked aside from the window.

"Stand still or I'll shoot!" The man's voice ordered.

Wentworth shoved aside the dog, charged toward the voice. His shoulder struck something yielding that grunted. He clasped his arms tight about the man and they slammed to the floor.

The man panted out a "Help!" that was breathless and scarcely audible. Wentworth's swift hand found the gun, wrenched it away from him. He flicked on the light and stared at his capture. The man was scrawny and frightened, his thin shanks shivering beneath the split tails of an old-fashioned night shirt.

Wentworth felt a pang of pity for the trembling man, but he had no time to indulge his compassion. He bound him swiftly, stripped a court plaster gag over his mouth and herded him into a closet. The dog still yapping ineffectually at his heels, he strode to the window and shut it, drew the shade. He carried the girl to the bath, began to bathe her throat and temples with cold water. There was spirits of ammonia in the medicine cabinet and he poured a dose into her mouth.

After ten minutes of persistent effort, the girl opened her

eyes dazedly. It would be two hours before she was normal, but she was at least conscious.

"What's your name?" Wentworth demanded swiftly. "Where do you live?"

The girl's eyes widened, still dazed.

"Hurry!" Wentworth snapped at her. "You're being framed for murder!"

The girl's mouth dropped open. She swallowed noisily. Wentworth poured another dose of ammonia down her throat.

"Come on," he said briskly. "You'll have to talk fast. What's your name?"

The girl finally mouthed out: "Grace Puystan."

Wentworth stared at her face intently. Recognition touched his mind. This girl was the debutante daughter of one of the wealthiest families in the country. And the gang had intended to frame her for murder! He frowned. What purpose could the dope ring possibly have? The girl's head sagged once more. Wentworth started to arouse her, but desisted. He could delay no longer. Police must already have started a room-by-room canvass of the building.

He crossed to the window, peered cautiously below. Two men prowled the areaway with groping lights. He whirled back to the room and the dog growled at him in treble. Wentworth looked down at it, and as he inspected the shaggy poodle with its puzzled, red-rimmed eyes, he smiled slowly.

HE POUNDED to the bathroom. A few moments' work with cold cream from the medicine cabinet stripped the make-up from his face. His hair, dried now, no longer plastered to his

24

head, he made gray with a dusting of powder. His hands flew, graying his complexion, distorting his fine strong face with lines of age.

Hurriedly he ripped off his clothing, darted into the next room and found a suit of his prisoner's clothes. The trousers exposed his ankles, and the coat was two inches short at the wrists. When he hunched his shoulders and perched a too small hat on his head, Wentworth was forced to grin at his own reflection. He was the image of a comic-strip henpecked husband.

The poodle followed him in resentful silence. When Wentworth turned toward the dog now, it eyed him suspiciously but did not renew its yapping, undoubtedly partly reassured by the scent of its master's clothes. Wentworth tossed a hundred dollar bill to the bed. He snapped the dog's leash to its collar, crossed swiftly to the girl. He could no longer carry her with him, lest she imperil his entire battle against the gang whose activities were beginning to amaze even the Spider. At least, she was out of the frame-up. There was no way now that those gangsters upstairs could involve her in the murder. He picked up an umbrella and turned to the now supercilious poodle. Wentworth's shoulders hunched timorously.

"Come on, Mimi," he said mildly. "Mama says you gotta go for a walk."

He walked downstairs three flights, almost bumped into a big-chested policeman on the first floor. He looked up at him with a frightened rabbit glance and said, "Oh, I beg your pardon. I'm so sorry. I didn't see you there." His voice was humble and apologetic.

"Where the hell do you think you're going?" The cop's voice thundered.

"I'm taking Mimi for a walk," Wentworth explained in his mild, frightened accents.

The cop's face was contemptuous. Amusement flickered in his eyes. "You skedaddle back up those steps," he ordered, "and don't stir out of your apartment until we find out where the Spider is. They think he went up on the roof."

Wentworth blinked up at the cop, and fright grew upon his face. "I can't go back up there. I can't!"

"Afraid of the Spider, huh?"

"Ye-e-es," Wentworth agreed slowly. "Yes, I'm afraid of the Spider," he went on volubly. "But that isn't it. My wife told me to take Mimi for a walk."

The cop was enjoying himself hugely now. "What, you'd leave your wife alone, with the Spider in the building? Don't you know that the Spider kills everybody he meets?"

Wentworth shook his head sadly. "You don't know my wife," he said. "Listen, Mr. Policeman, I *gotta* take Mimi out for a walk."

"Gotta? What do you mean, gotta?"

Wentworth glanced up at him quickly, looked down at the floor again in obvious embarrassment.

"Well, you see," said Wentworth slowly, "this is Mimi's regular time to go out and she hasn't been out since this afternoon, and my wife said to take her for a walk..." His voice trailed off.

"Yeah? Well, you tell your wife I say you can't go."

Wentworth raised his head eagerly. "You come up and tell

her. It'll be all right if you tell her. But she won't believe me. Come on," Wentworth turned toward the stairs. "Come on, Mr. Policeman, you tell her."

The cop shook his head, retreated a pace. "Not me," he said. "I got a wife."

"Oh, but I can't do it." Wentworth was agitated now. "I can't go back and tell her that Mimi—that Mimi… Officer, Mimi has *gotta* go out."

The cop stared at him for a moment, opened his mouth, closed it again. "Aw, get the hell out of here with your Mimi," he ordered gruffly. "But come right back as soon as—as soon as—Come right back."

"Thank you, sir. Thank you, sir. You're very kind," Wentworth babbled. "Come along, Mimi."

He led the supercilious poodle toward the exit. But as he reached it, the door was thrust open and a woman waddled in. She stared at Wentworth suspiciously. Her eyes narrowed at sight of the hat, then jerked to the dog. Dismay squeaked from her. She snatched the poodle, spotted the policeman.

"Officer," she demanded stridently, "arrest this man! He was stealing my precious little Tootsie."

CHAPTER 3
MURDER—IN JOB LOTS

THE POLICEMAN'S mouth fell open, his eyes bulged and his hand snapped toward his gun. Wentworth ducked out the door, crossed the pavement in two bounds to the jumble

RICHARD WENTWORTH

of radio police cars parked at the curb. The policeman, gun raised, smacked the apartment doors open, plunged out. Wentworth threw his umbrella like a harpoon. It speared between the cop's legs.

He cursed, floundered. As he pitched to the sidewalk, gun flying wide, Wentworth sprang into a police car and hurled it forward with roaring motor. He spun a corner on two moaning tires before the cop behind scrambled to his feet.

Two minutes later, when Wentworth abandoned the radio car and climbed calmly into his own Lancia behind Ram Singh, police auto sirens were whining all about like hungry dogs that have lost a scent. But no policeman challenged the majestic limousine slipping through traffic with a dark-visaged Hindu at the wheel.

Once clear, Wentworth drew the shades and pressed a button concealed beneath the edge of the left half of the seat. The seat slid forward, revolved and revealed a complete wardrobe of clothing in its back, a mirror illuminated by a shielded light and toilet and make-up articles in a tray. Swiftly Wentworth donned his habitual attire of dark tweeds, removed the makeup of age from his tanned face.

Five minutes later, he pressed the button again; the seat slid

back into place, and Richard Wentworth rolled through the upper west side in his limousine. He picked up the speaking tube.

"The home of the *Missie Sahib,*" he ordered.

The Lancia swung west to Riverside Drive, paralleled the Hudson with its distant gleaming lights along the Palisades that the Missie Sahib, who was Wentworth's fiancée, Nita van Sloan, loved to paint. At the Riverside Towers, Ram Singh halted.

"Wait," Wentworth ordered briefly, and entered, nodding to the bowing *chasseur.* A hall-boy phoned to Miss van Sloan's apartment and when Wentworth left the elevator on the top floor, Nita's door was open and Nita, smiling and charming in a black and white frock, held out a white hand to him. Her Great Dane dog, Apollo, thrust out his head, barked a low welcome.

The door closed behind them, and Wentworth took Nita tenderly in his arms. He gazed down into her warm blue eyes, touched the chestnut and gold of her curling locks. The girl's smile faded.

"Whom are you fighting now, Dick?" she asked quietly, and led him to a seat beside windows that showed, far below, the black waters of the river, black with trails of wavering golden-light.

Wentworth's smile faded too. It was at once the great joy and the great grief of his life, his love for Nita. The grief was frequent and the joy rare.

For the life of Richard Wentworth was not his own. It was

dedicated to his ceaseless battle against crime, and the hourly risk of death was his. Their love was one more of his sacrifices upon the altar of justice and service to humanity. For Wentworth felt that no man had a right to marry, to have a family, when his life was forfeit in advance to Death; when the Law had a claim upon him for the many he had slain, even though all had been killed in the name of justice.

And his very love for Nita was in itself a grave danger to the girl. More than once some ruthless Underworld opponent had struck at him through his love for Nita, the one woman in the world whom he had trusted with the truth of his identity; the one woman who knew that the wealthy young clubman, sportsman and dilettante of the arts, Richard Wentworth, was the Spider.

Wentworth threw off his gloomy thoughts. He did not regret his life, hard though it was. Nita, too, had dedicated herself to the service of humanity and justice. And the service was worthy. He smiled slowly again into Nita's eyes.

"You always know, don't you, darling?" His smile turned into grim resolve; his strong face became lean-jawed with determination; his gray-blue eyes glinted. He told Nita briefly what had happened, of Grace Puystan, doped and scheduled to be framed for murder, then asked her to arrange for them to visit the girl's home.

"I'm going to Washington tonight," he told her, "to follow up this white-haired gangster who wore the bloody serpent and to tip off the department of justice that the gangs of New York and Washington, perhaps of the entire nation, have turned to narcotics."

He looked steadily into Nita's eyes. The Great Dane thrust its big head into his lap and he fondled it absently. "Do you realize, Nita, what gang dissemination of dope means? Have you ever seen a drug addict?"

Nita shook her chestnut curls slowly, her eyes grave upon his.

WENTWORTH LEANED forward, elbows on his knees. His strong brown fingers clenched. "I saw a girl brought into Bellevue recently," he said slowly. "She had been a lovely thing… *had been*. Her face was distorted almost to bestiality. Her lips drooled. Her eyes—they had seen hell.

"She was of good family, but through dope she had drifted into association with the vilest element in the world. Through immorality, through increasing usage of drugs, her mind had cracked. She had become a hemophile, a lover of blood. She was taken to Bellevue when the howling of a dog drew police to the hovel where she lived. She had tied the dog, up and was slicing it to pieces slowly with a knife. She wanted to see the blood….

"That's what dope can do. Take that case, multiply it by hundreds, thousands. The young women, the future mothers of our nation, the young men who would be its backbone! By God, Nita, the very life of the country is threatened!"

He jerked to his feet, stood with clenched fists, staring out into the black night.

"It is a good fight," said Nita quietly.

32

The tension went out of Wentworth. He took Nita in his arms and pressed her red lips to his. "You are my main strength, dear," he said quietly. "You give me courage to keep on." Then his voice grew crisp. "I'm going to phone Tom Inverness, in the District Attorney's office, and see that the city is warned what threatens."

"Can't you get hold of Kirkpatrick?"

Wentworth shook his head, striding toward the phone. The police commissioner was the one to notify, but Wentworth knew that at that moment he was aboard a plane, flying back from a short, much-needed vacation in the South. And the Spider couldn't wait. In the morning he must be in Washington.

Inverness' voice came to him heavily over the wires.

"It's Wentworth calling," said the Spider. "Do you know, Tom, that the gangs have turned to narcotics as a racket?"

"Do I know it?" muttered Inverness. "The whole department is honeycombed with graft because of it. You don't know the half of it!"

There was a cold venom in his voice that tightened Wentworth's gaze. "Just what do you mean?" he asked softly.

"Haven't you heard about Porter and Tugwell and Pearson?" Inverness demanded sharply.

"No," said Wentworth. "No. I've been busy recently and haven't been much out in society."

Inverness laughed bitterly. "You might not have heard, even so," he said. "Porter is supposed to have had a nervous break down. Actually, he went crazy from taking dope. He was worth millions. Now his wife and his three kids are penniless, living on relatives. A stranger got all his money, in some devious way that leaves us with absolutely no evidence of actual crime."

Wentworth's voice was heavy. "No suspects? Not even a hunch?" he asked hopefully.

"No," said Inverness shortly. "But...."

"The gangs are operating on a national, perhaps an international scale," Wentworth cut in. "I know they have a branch in Washington."

"That's where they got Pearson," said Inverness. "Hadn't you heard of his suicide?"

"I hadn't heard," Wentworth admitted woodenly. "Pearson was one of the finest minds in economic research in the country. Was that dope, too?"

"That was dope," was the succinct answer. "He found himself addicted, left a rambling note accusing some woman of introducing him to it, and shot himself."

There was a white rage within Wentworth now. If the menace of wholesale distribution of dope had seemed enormous to him before, it now had become terrible beyond all reckoning. Two of his own friends, one a millionaire, the other a recognized economist of wide repute, victims of the drug habit....

He squeezed out a curse between locked teeth.

"And Tugwell?" he asked in a strained voice.

"Missing," said Inverness laconically. "We found a cache of cocaine in his home. Why should a psychiatrist of his reputation, with his knowledge of the consequences, take up narcotics?"

"God knows," said Wentworth grimly, "but that's one of the things I intend to find out. If this damnable Bloody Serpent can strike those three, no one is safe. The President of the United States himself, all our big men might be victimized—driven to insanity and death!" Wentworth cut himself off. "Here are things to investigate, Inverness," he said. "Last night's activities of Big Mick Harrigan; the restaurant of Nino Carlotti on West...."

"I know Carlotti. Is he mixed up in it?"

"I think he's a victim," Wentworth said shortly. "I'll tell you more tomorrow. I've got to hurry now."

He spun from the phone, caught Nita once more into his arms, "I'll be back from Washington in the afternoon," he said, and he was gone.

THE LANCIA sped him to Pennsylvania station just in time for the twelve-thirty train. In Washington, at the Department of Justice from which he held special powers, he learned other things that locked his jaw in grim determination to strike swiftly at the spreading menace of the gangs. He learned that the attack was nationwide, that in every corner of the country, from the Mexican border to Canada, from Pacific to storm-lashed Atlantic, narcotic agents reported a terrible—unstoppable stream of narcotics pouring into the country, unstoppable because the gangs had struck fearfully and without warning at the enforcement army. A pitifully small army it was, two hundred sixty men—and the gang's weapon was murder.

In some fiendish way, they had learned the identities of a hundred of the narcotic army—and a hundred men had been murdered! Knifed in their beds, shot down on the streets....

Jim Hendricks, the square-jawed chief of the narcotic division, tossed a yellow oblong of paper, a telegram, on the desk before Wentworth. It was in code, words penciled below the symbols on the sheet.

FOUND BADGES AND GUNS OF SMITH AND
BEAUNE IN LIME KILN HERE ANALYSIS SHOWS
BODIES DESTROYED BY QUICK LIME
C 17

"That makes one hundred and two dead," the chief said heavily, his thick hand a fist on the desk. "Smith and Beaune were two of my best men. They had discovered some valuable lead at Buffalo, proof that great operations were under way, but nothing to show definitely who was the head of them. C 17— that's Grayson—is coming here today. He's due now, as a matter of fact, to tell what he knows. We can't trust the code any longer." The fist slammed the desk. "Damn them! They're crippling my force."

Wentworth still stared at the telegram. Murdered, their bodies destroyed in quick lime. Another horror added to the transcendent tearfulness of dope and its victims.

"But more men can be enlisted," he muttered.

"They are being enlisted," Hendricks said shortly, "but they must be trained. I have an appropriation, to double the force. That will be done. Meantime, my best men have been killed." He paused. "Twenty others have resigned. I can't blame them."

Wentworth leaned forward, his jaw set. He gave what information he had and concluded: "Here in Washington, I believe a man is operating who will answer this description."

He gave a detailed *portrait parlait* of the gangster he had struck down in the New York apartment. As he spoke, a peculiar expression came into Chief Hendricks' face.

"I have known you too long to question your accuracy, Dick," he said slowly, "but what you say is—" he shook his head.

"You know the man?" Wentworth snapped out.

Hendricks, unsmiling, pressed a white button in a row of four on his desk and ordered, "file 342 of photographs." When the big brown envelope was placed before him, he tossed a picture before Wentworth, eyes intent on his face.

"That's the man," said Wentworth. "Who is it?"

Chief Hendricks frowned. "That's my strongest advocate with the government," he said, "—Senator Tarleton Bragg!"

WENTWORTH'S LIPS grew thin. "Nevertheless," he snapped out, "I suggest that you check on his alibi for last night. There's something damned fishy about this." The eyes of the two men met firmly. "I've got to get back to New York. If I learn anything further, I'll let you know. In the meantime I'd appreciate any new information you unearth at this end."

The chief nodded. "You'll get it." He stood up, and their hand clasp was firm. Wentworth strode from the office, descended three floors, and moved rapidly along the high echoing corridor toward the bright daylight of the exit. He was thinking swiftly. A leak in the Department of Justice, while not impossible, was extremely unlikely….

On Pennsylvania Avenue, Wentworth hailed a taxi and began

to cruise slowly through the neighborhood, noting the license numbers of the cars they passed. In three quarters of an hour, they passed one cab three times, and always it was traveling past the entrance of the Treasury Annex, where Hendricks had his office.

Wentworth left his taxi, hailed another and ordered it to follow the cab he had spotted three times. As he trailed, the car ahead swerved to the curb at the signal of a young woman, and Wentworth, eyeing her, smiled slowly. He recognized that too-tight, slightly theatrical manner of dress, the silk sheath that, black this time, outlined the girl's shapely body, the blonde hair fluffing from beneath a close hat. It was Tess Goodleigh, the girl whose gun he had used to kill two gangsters in New York!

His own cab circled the block swiftly, whirled back in front of the Treasury Annex building. A party of men was gaping up in front of it. Another man, gaunt and tanned, strode long-legged along the sidewalk. The girl's cab swerved to the curb beside him.

The sightseers seemed to blunder into the tall man's path. One of them spoke to him, pointing his hand toward the Treasury Annex. The gaunt man shook his head, raised his arm to point south along the street toward the main treasury building.

The sightseers were all about him now. He stood out like a tall pine amid scrub bushes. He flung a single swift glance about him. The men crowded closer. The man's shoulders braced angrily, but he walked slowly along with the men, in the direction he had pointed, toward Pennsylvania Avenue.

Wentworth tapped on the glass, halted his cab to watch the slowly walking group. The men seemed in no hurry, talked among themselves, laughed and peered at the buildings on all sides. They crossed Pennsylvania, turned into the White House park, Wentworth following at a distance. He saw them enter two parked cars, taking the tall men with them, and a grim, ugly light glinted in Wentworth's eyes.

A man had been kidnapped from in front of the Treasury Annex building in Washington, snatched from the doorstep of the chief to whom he was going to report! For Wentworth was positive that the tall man was Grayson, coming to tell Hendricks of the Buffalo gangsters—of the death of his two comrades!

CHAPTER 4
THE QUICKLIME PIT

THROUGH BRIGHT morning sunshine that seemed a mockery, the three cars, two limousines with their murderous gang, and Wentworth in the taxi, sped along the river bank, whirled out onto the low-lying Alexandria bridge and shot toward the wooded hills of Virginia. Less than twenty miles beyond that bridge, the limousines whirled into a grassy lane.

Wentworth dared not follow there. He sent his taxi past the lane, stopped around the next wooded bend and paid off the driver.

"Get the police," Wentworth told him. "Those men are kidnapers."

The driver's eyes narrowed. "Right!" he snapped out.

Smiling thinly, Wentworth watched him drive away, fast. Only a moment he stood so, then sped light-footed through the woodland. Above him trees were bright with the new greenery of May. The twittering of birds was everywhere. Ahead was death.

A hundred yards from the road a clearing broke the woods and Wentworth crouched in underbrush at its edge. A weathered farmhouse squatted on the slope of the hill. Below and behind it, stood a dilapidated red barn. The two limousines Wentworth had trailed were parked before the house. As Wentworth watched, the gangsters, with their towering prisoner, debouched behind the building and moved in a compact group, like some loathsome many-legged beast, toward the barn whose ancient beams had rotted until, lop-sided, it leaned downhill.

Quickly Wentworth circled through the woods until the house was between himself and the lopsided barn, then sprinted across the clearing to the limousines.

He searched the cars, found keys were in one and pocketed them. Then he moved alertly to a corner of the farmhouse. No one was in sight in the gaping doors of the barn, though he could make out shadows within the dusty shafts of sunlight that filtered through the broken roof. A swift, soundless sprint placed him beside the barn.

Within, voices rumbled. One rose clear and firm.

"You can do what you damned please with me," it stated angrily. "I won't talk."

Laughter that Wentworth recognized, answered that defiance, laughter of the Man of the White Muffler, the man of the Bloody Serpent Ring, he whom Hendricks had identified as Senator Tarleton Bragg!

Soft words followed that soft laughter: "Won't you say? Then it is a matter of will. I have ways of breaking a man's will." The hissing of the laughter sounded again. "Take off his shoes and socks. You see, my dear C 17, we do not have to *throw* you into the quicklime, we can dip your feet and legs, appropriately weighted, into the pit. The screams of others have testified that it is quite painful."

THE SPIDER'S hand closed upon his gun. Deftly he slipped on the black-skirted mask. Then, poised for battle, he hesitated. All sound had ceased within the barn, all sound except furtive whispers.

Wentworth whirled and darted away, zigzagging frantically. So swiftly had he interpreted that silence, so quickly had he acted, that he was three quarters of the way to the farmhouse before the first gangster darted into the open with blazing gun.

Wentworth whirled the corner of the house, jerked himself to a halt with an outflung hand. His gun spat down the slope, and the gangster in the doorway jerked out of his crouch, stiffened into rigid death by that winging bullet.

A fusillade blasted through the gaping door of the barn. Lead tore the farmhouse, spun brittle yellow splinters into the air. But no more gangsters showed.

41

Wentworth wheeled from the corner. It would be suicide to continue this futile duel until the gangsters could slip away behind the barn, or send a circling gunman to take him from the rear. He sprang to the gang car to which he had no keys. Swiftly binding its steering wheel in place with his belt, he bent his whipcord strength to the task and started it rolling.

The nose of the car thrust out from behind the corner of the farmhouse. A burst of shots greeted it. The running board grated against wood, wedged it stationary. With frantic haste, Went-

The car, traveling at the rate of fifty miles an
hour, crashed into the side of the old barn.

worth leaped to the driver's seat of the second car, started it and
slammed its nose against the first limousine's rear bumper. With
a ripping burst of wood, the wedged car tore lose, bumped over
a shallow ditch and rolled gently down grade toward the barn.

Men showed momentarily within the barn, darting across
the beams of sunlight. Wentworth held his fire, crouching low
behind the wheel of the second gang car. The limousine ahead
gained speed. It struck a rock and bounced high, lunged on as
if eagerly. A gangster, panic-stricken, flung from the doorway.
The Spider's gun spat, and the man slapped down on his face
with a scream.

Ahead, the driverless juggernaut flung on, bounding over
hummocks, careening wildly. From the far side of the barn came

the smashing of wood as men sought to escape from that plunging battering ram of death and the mortal bullets of the Spider.

Wentworth's lips twisted in a thin smile. He heard the shouted threats of the leader as he tried to hold his men steady.

But the Spider gave the leader no chance to rally his men. In the wake of the wildly dashing limousine, he tooled the second gang car. The windshield would shed bullets like rain, he knew. The driverless car bounded forward at fully fifty miles an hour down the increasing grade. With a final mad plunge, it struck a hummock and vaulted like a horse at a hurdle. Its full three-ton weight, reinforced by the momentum of its fifty-mile pace, slammed into the side of the dilapidated barn with a crash like the day of Judgment.

IT WAS over in a flash. One instant the leaping limousine was poised in the air, hurtling toward the side of the barn. The next it had vanished amid a tearing explosion of sound, and there was a gaping hole in the red painted side.

Screams came from within, high-pitched, mortal. A second ripping blast of ancient wood told that the car smashed through the far wall. Wentworth stepped on the gas.

Sunlight pouring through the splintered side showed a man stretched motionless on the ground, but it was not from him the brain-searing screams came. They continued, cries of clear, insupportable agony. The barn tottered, trembling in every timber. Slowly its list downhill increased. Wentworth sent the second car careening madly down the hummocked slope.

"Grayson!" he shouted. "Grayson! To me!"

A man plunged from the barn, but he was short, one of the gangsters. Wentworth's gun spat death.

"Grayson!" he cried again.

Another figure dived from blackness into golden sunlight, a man with one foot bare, a man gaunt and tall. This was Grayson. A gun crashed out behind him. He pitched to the earth, rolled, sprang up and raced on toward Wentworth.

Again the gun within vomited sound and flame. Grayson went down hard, he tried to rise, but the effort was feeble. Wentworth slowed his car, swerved it, brought it to a skidding stop between Grayson and the barn. Wentworth sprang out beside him.

As if in echo of that final shot that had felled Grayson, the barn sagged with a blasting burst of timbers, canted downgrade at a sharper angle and collapsed, crashing into a jumbled mass of wreckage. Its fall shut off the cries within like the closing of a soundproof door.

Wentworth's ears gave him the record of what was happening, but he paid no heed. He caught up the wounded Grayson, lifted him into the tonneau of the limousine and whirled, gun ready, toward the collapsed barn.

From it came no shots, no sounds. Movement jerked Wentworth's eyes beyond it. The limousine he had sent as a torpedo against the gangster fortress was still moving, but now it rolled slowly, cautiously, and there was a guiding hand at the wheel. Two men were in it. The car was battered, but even as Wentworth watched, the motor roared out and it shot along a narrow, grass grown roadway that writhed like a snake up the far slope.

"Go on," urged a weak voice behind Wentworth. "Go on. Kill the last one of the rats."

The Spider turned his masked face toward Grayson. The agent's straining hands gripped the back of the car's front seat. His face was white with pain. Once more he gasped out, "Go on!" then slumped from sight. Wentworth sprang to the limousine. Grayson was bleeding badly from a wound in his right side.

Lips tight, Wentworth ripped his clothing aside, made an emergency dressing to contain the hemorrhage. If the agent was to survive, if Hendricks was to get the information, he must be rushed to a hospital.

The Spider paused for only one thing, as the gang car vanished over the next hill. He darted to the body of the nearest gangster, searched him swiftly but in vain for a serpent ring, and imprinted upon his forehead the seal of the Spider.

Rapidly he went from man to man, searching and leaving always his ugly, threatening red card of death. In the ruins of the barn, he found two bodies and all that was left of a third man, a hand that reached from a pit of quicklime, a hand that, pinned to the ground by a fallen beam, was attached to no body.

The smile that wrenched at Wentworth's lips was mocking. The lime pit made for Grayson had taken toll of its creators. Quickly Wentworth fixed his red seal upon the hand also and sped back to the car, wrenched it about and sent it swiftly back toward a farmhouse, out upon the highway. Far up the road he saw speeding cars. That would be the police. At least they could be counted upon to speed Grayson to the hospital. Wentworth halted the car in the middle of the road, ducked into the woods and made a rapid and soundless retreat through the sun-dappled trees.

CHAPTER 5
THE SERPENT'S
CRIMSON TRAIL

S HORT HOURS after, the plane that was carrying Wentworth homeward came down at Newark airport. Nita met him, and the two of them settled into the Lancia's deep cushions behind the competently broad shoulders of Jackson, his chauffeur. When Ram Singh had mounted to the seat beside the driver and the car had nosed forward into the heavy, trans-meadow traffic, Wentworth turned to Nita.

"Darling," he told her grimly, "if those gangsters in Washington are alive to their job—and I think they are—they will discover that one Richard Wentworth trailed them from Hendricks' office. And when they find that trail ended with the seal of the Spider on the bodies of their gunmen, they'll come gunning for me.... Gangsters aren't like the police. They need only suspicions before they strike, not proof."

The perfect oval of Nita's face was grave. "Perhaps we'd better call off that visit to Grace Puystan's home, then," she said slowly. "We're invited there this evening." A slight smile lifted the corners of her red mouth. "The invitations are labeled M.I.S.T.B.D."

"Which means?" queried Wentworth.

"Make it smart to be dopey!"

Wentworth's lips became a straight, thin line. "So that's why the gangsters wanted to frame Grace Puystan for murder!" he said softly, "She's to make narcotics popular in the smart set! God above! Where will this gang stop?" His eyes glinted. "We can look for fun—and danger—at Grace Puystan's this evening."

Wentworth took Nita to her home and set out at once for the restaurant of Nino Carlotti, with its swanky, tree-sentineled entrance and its gorgeously clad doorman. The *maitre d'hotel* bowed as obsequiously as ever, but when Wentworth asked for Carlotti, his face became wooden, as expressionless as his bald head with its single curled strand of black hair.

"Mr. Carlotti no longer owns the *Dry Club*, Mr. Wentworth," he said.

Wentworth raised his brows. "Who is the new owner?"

"Mr. Terence Harrigan, sir," Wentworth frowned.

So the Big Mick himself had calmly taken over poor Carlotti's lucrative business. He scarcely heeded the head waiter's murmured invitation to be seated and served. Finally he caught the man's words, jerked a negative. "No, I wanted to see Carlotti personally. Know where he can be reached?"

The maître d'hotel's smile was wintry. "The morning papers, sir, say he has been arrested because the Spider killed two men in his apartment."

"In his apartment!" the words were pulled out of Wentworth, then he shrugged. "I didn't identify that Carlotti with Nino," he said, nodded and went out. He took a taxi directly to the Tombs prison where, after some difficulty, he managed an interview with Carlotti. He took his seat on one side of the wire mesh that divided the visitor's room and studied the man. Carlotti, opposite him, was broken. His fat hands massaged each other without ceasing.

"What happened, Nino," Wentworth asked in kindly tones. "I hear Harrigan muscled in on your restaurant."

The man glanced about in fright, found only the guard's eyes upon him and whispered in a voice that was scarcely audible.

"He did, sir, only in the name of the Blessed Virgin, do not permit…."

Wentworth's short nod cut him short. "Tell me about it," he said briskly.

Carlotti's hands tore themselves apart for an instant. He gestured outward with palms up so violently that his fat quivered. "He just walked in and told me he was taking it over."

"*What?*"

Carlotti's hands grasped each other again, made washing movements. "Yes, that was it."

"But you called the police!"

Carlotti nodded. His third chin squeezed out over his collar. "I got hold of Geraghty, on the beat; an honest cop he is, too, Harrigan laughed at him! And when Geraghty pulled his gun, two of Harrigan's men took it away from him."

Wentworth's eyes narrowed. "And did you call his superiors?"

Carlotti nodded slowly. "They cursed me and told me they couldn't be bothered with civil matters. They said if I paid Harrigan what I owed him, he couldn't serve the attachment."

He lifted his heavy shoulders in a shrug. "I don't owe Harrigan anything, and they know it. It is what you call a dodge."

"Did you stop there?" Wentworth demanded angrily.

"But it was useless, *Signor* Wentworth! If the police are corrupt... and besides, they pricked me with a needle that made me forget. Until today, I have not known what happens. And today I am crazy. I want that needle." His nervousness increased. "Could you, *Signor*, obtain for me one little prick of that needle that brings forgetfulness, just one, *Signor!*" His face twitched. His fingers on the wire mesh were like fat claws....

DUSK WAS blackening the streets, dotted with yellow lights, when Wentworth strode from the gray stone pile of the city jail.

"West 47th Street police station," he ordered Jackson.

But Geraghty, off duty, had donned civilian clothes and taken himself off on some private errand, the sergeant told Wentworth at the station.

"And where would that be?" Wentworth asked.

The sergeant shrugged, eyes opaque and suspicious.

"How do I know?" he demanded.

"Do you think if I called Stanley Kirkpatrick, you could remember?" Wentworth demanded. His voice was soft, but there was a glint in his eyes. The sergeant stared at him, hesitated a moment, then got out a surly "guess" that Geraghty was at Chowder Sam's. "There's a party on there tonight, and Geraghty thinks the guy who took his gun may be there."

Wentworth jerked a nod. Chowder Sam's. He knew that place, too, as indeed he knew almost every hangout of gangster and crook in the city. Chowder Sam's, a big, sprawling room half underground, with a hundred curtained alcoves, a dozen "back rooms" and two floors to which rickety stairs led above.

A man could place a bet for a hundred grand at Sam's and not achieve so much as the flicker of an eye lash in recognition; or he could find a game of "penny ante" and might or might not come away with his life.

Yes, the Spider knew Chowder Sam's. Richard Wentworth could not go there, but a Cockney deck steward off the Franconia, his shore clothes greasy and wrinkled after three months on the beach....

A nearby second-hand clothes shop, a subway station washroom, and Wentworth had vanished. In his stead stood Snuffer Dan Tewkes, a stoop-shouldered man in coat and trousers that did not match, with a lax mouth that quirked upward loosely at one corner when he smiled. The bridge of his nose was thick, as thought it had been broken, and his speech was continually interrupted by loud snuffing of breath through the smashed nasal chambers. This was the man that, an hour later, shuffled down Chowder Sam's garish stairway into the big room with its gleaming bar and curtained alcoves.

He sidled up to the bar. "Whisky and soda," he ordered, his voice as Cockney as Limehouse. He snuffed loudly.

The barkeep had a classic roach of black hair that curled smoothly back from his forehead. "Go sit down. Go sit down!" he growled. "Don't you know nothin'?"

During two drinks of bad scotch, Wentworth noted that more than half those who entered, men and a sprinkling of women, filtered ultimately through curtains that seemed only those of another alcove. But enough people went through that entrance to pack a dozen alcoves to overflowing. When a group of five men walked slowly across the room and headed toward the curtains, Wentworth attached himself inconspicuously to its outskirts and filed through with them. Aside from that masked door, no precaution was taken. And in the back room, drinks were sloshed across the bar, and something else that tightened Wentworth's anger within him; small white packets that he recognized, "decks" of dope. Narcotics passed as freely across the bar as liquor in a pre-repeal speakeasy!

Wentworth sauntered up to the bar, got his whisky and soda and, gripping the glass, turned his back to the bar, hooked his elbows upon it. He smiled tipsily outward at the swelling crowd. His glance was casual, but keenly attentive. No one watching him could have known the anger that burned within him as a slow fire, gnawing at him, mounting until hot flames seemed to leap to his brain. For about him he saw the ravages of the drug, saw corruption seeping not into criminal lives, but into those of the steadfast, plodding middle class upon which the strength of the nation rested.

There was Bill, night man at the garage where Wentworth kept his cars. A reliable sort, was Bill, supporting, besides a wife and two children an infirm mother. Wentworth had always been particularly liberal with him, knowing the money went to good usage. Now—Wentworth peered with bitter eyes—Bill was dancing a hot and close step with a girl whose body, silk sheathed and swaying, was the sensual personification of the evil of the drugs. There was a feverish light in Bill's eyes, and his mouth was twisted.

THE ENTIRE crowd was made up of men like that, Wentworth could see clerks from offices; skilled workmen who had struggled upward a little way along the ladder to prosperity. Not one was inherently vicious, but under the burning prod of the narcotics, these, too, would be corrupted, turned to crime or violence. Their morals would be undermined, their minds weakened, their years of patient toil sacrificed…. Everywhere the thin packets of hell-powder were being dealt out. Some were paid for, some not.

Wentworth cursed under his breath, turned to the bar and ordered another drink. He picked up his glass and moved vaguely off toward the darker corners. Somewhere in this mad mêlée was the policeman who had sought to help Nino Carlotti, hoping to bring to book the men who had humiliated him.

A burst of shouting from a dark corner, and four men reeled out into the brighter lights with a fifth struggling among them.

"Hey, look what we found!" One of the captors sang out. "Here's a copper!"

The man who struggled among them, face congested with dark, angry blood, wore his shield upon his vest and his coat had been torn almost from him.

Bill, the garage man Wentworth had known, spun his dancing partner away from him, snatched up a drink and dashed it into the face of the struggling policeman whom, Wentworth knew, could be none other than Geraghty.

"Kill the cop!" shouted Bill.

A heavy man who moved with a gliding ease thrust between the policeman and the crowd. The mob snarled like defeated wolves. The man raised his hands, palms toward the crowd, and smiled oily.

"My friends," he called. "My friends!"

"Let us at him, Sam!"

"My friends!"

A muttering quiet fell upon the crowd. Chowder Sam pivoted, his raised palms spreading the hush. When finally he could make his voice heard, he shouted:

"I do not blame you, my friends, for being angry." Growls interrupted him. His frown brought quiet. "I do not blame you. You are right to think that this policeman should be punished."

Shouts and shaken fists. The crowd strained closer. It took Chowder Sam two minutes of patting the air with fat palms to still them.

"But," he said, "he is to be punished only for his daring to come here in an unfriendly way. The police are our friends. There is not one in ten who is not with us."

"That's a lie!" shouted Geraghty.

SAM TURNED toward him suavely. "It is the truth," he said. "Why can't you be our friend, too? We made you an offer. Instead of taking it like a wise man, you get hard with us." He shook his head slowly, his eyes never leaving Geraghty's. "It doesn't pay to get hard with us, to come around spying...."

Once more the crowd shouted, cried that Geraghty should die, that he be hanged, shot, poisoned. Chowder Sam, smiling as beneficently as a parson, turned to face them again, patting the air.

"I suggest!" he shouted. "I suggest!" and the turmoil stilled. "I suggest that Patrolman Geraghty, just to show he bears us no ill will should take—" he paused and even the restless muttering of the crowd died— "should take a sniff of the joy powder, too!"

"Yeah!" yelled the crowd. "That's the stuff!"

Clerks who bowed servilely before their bosses in daylight hours performed a crazy war dance of excitement. Bill, the garage man, loosed a roar of approval, shaking hard fists above his head. Women touched tongues to their rouged and feverish lips.

Sam stepped aside. The policeman was rigid with anger.

"Will you join us, my friend?" asked Sam suavely.

"I will not!" the cop bit out.

Sam reached into his inside pocket and flourished on high a glittering needle. He turned toward the policeman while men and women danced and yelled behind him in a bestial saturnalia. No one saw Wentworth's arm slide across a table to a light, saw his knife slash through wires so that they sparked with blue white flame. They only saw darkness fall like a black storm upon the room, heard the crazy bedlam that it brought. WENTWORTH WAS across the floor in two bounds. He collided with a man and sent him sprawling. He reached the tight group that surrounded the policeman and his ramming impetus slammed him through it and into Geraghty's captors.

Wentworth struck swiftly with scientific fists. Men grunted and went down.

"Geraghty!" Wentworth whispered, heard the policeman's panting answer as he struggled also for freedom. "There's a door in the back."

Groping, he found the battling center of the storm, struck twice and heard a man stand panting beside him.

"Geraghty," he whispered again.

"Okay," said the cop. "Thanks, buddy."

His whistle bit the darkness, clapped back from the walls. Panic raised its ugly head. Men and women, crazed by drugs, fought in mad terror to escape. Once more Chowder Sam's voice rose calmly.

"My friends!" he cried. "My friends! Do not worry about the police. They are *our friends!*"

Geraghty cursed. Wentworth's hand on his shoulder stayed his charge toward that voice.

"Come away," Wentworth whispered. "Out the back door. Come, you've done all you can."

The shoulder still strained against his hand, but gradually tension went out of the policeman. He let Wentworth lead him backward. Flashlights began to poke the inquiring fingers of their beams over the crowd. Over in a corner a woman screamed and screamed.

Wentworth reached the door. A torch slammed its dazzling beam into his eyes. A gun belched flame. Geraghty grunted with pain, bent double. Wentworth jerked free his automatic, fired above the eye of the light.

The torch fell and Wentworth sprang forward. The light's crazy beam spotted Chowder Sam, face distorted, sliding weakly to the floor.

The light spilled across his dying face and glazing eyes. Wentworth's hand darted forward, touched the man's forehead, then he caught up Geraghty and, carrying the policeman bodily, sped down a dark passageway to the street, leaving behind him on the oily forehead of Chowder Sam, the Spider's token that he had struck once more in the battle against the Bloody Serpent, his ugly red, menacing seal!

Once out in the clean air of the night, Wentworth bent over Geraghty, feeling for the wound, for a pulse. He found the wound, but the heart was still. His lips formed a straight, bitter line as he stood erect. He had taken a life for a life, but the Bloody Serpent writhed on, stinging, spreading its subtle poison throughout the land, among the homes of the sturdy middle class, worming into the homes of the mighty....

CHAPTER 6
IT'S SMART TO BE DOPEY

THE HOMES of the mighty... Richard Wentworth, tall and irreproachable in evening dress, his Inverness cape with its white satin lining agleam, alighted from the Lancia and with Nita on his arm, sauntered into the reception room of the Puystans' Park Avenue apartment. Fun and danger, Wentworth had forecast for this night. But there was nothing to indicate that he feared danger with Nita—Nita of the brown clustering curls, Nita lovely in sequins and white chiffon—smiling beside him. The girl Wentworth had saved from a murder charge, Grace Puystan, bade them welcome. She walked aside with Nita, escorting her personally to the room reserved for the ladies' wraps.

Wentworth strolled off through the congested rooms, formal in gray and white, with divans and chairs along walls ornamented by high-hung, gold-framed paintings. He studied the people about him, boyish youths, débutante daughters of the wealthy.

Everywhere faces were flushed. The dancing was continuous and, rhythmed by a Negro orchestra, jerkily sensuous. Making a deft way across the floor toward the doorway of a shadowed conservatory that profiled potted palms with pointed, finger fronds, he noted several older men; Pelton Hobbs, a banker whom he knew; Conrad Burns, who idled for his living, and another man, massive-shouldered, with a knotted bulging forehead that dominated his entire face, that overshadowed the jovial, slightly heavy cheeks and the small bright eyes.

Wentworth nodded casually to Hobbs, offered his cigarette case of gleaming platinum and black enamel to Conrad Burns.

"Since when did you become one of the fast young set?" he asked laughingly.

Conrad Burns shrugged world-weary shoulders, smiled with a vacuity his keenly alive eyes did not echo. He murmured, "And yourself?"

"Friend of the family," Wentworth assured him. "I'm here to lend the party dignity."

"Dignity," murmured Burns and sniggered. Wentworth looked

at him sharply. Burns' pupils were distended. His eyes had a glazed, feverish look.

"Do you bring your own," Wentworth asked casually, "or is it passed out by the butler?"

"Oh, the butler," said Burns, then cut off with a jerk, shot a suspicious stare at Wentworth. A girl pranced by. A shoulder strap had slipped. As she waved a flirtatious hand at Burns, the other slid off also. She let them droop, accentuating her extremely low décolletage. She made a *moué* at Burns. He caught her hand, threw an arm about her lithesome waist and they skipped into the invitingly dim conservatory.

WENTWORTH'S EYES narrowed. His studied glance swept the room. Everywhere were signs of narcotics. Girls' mouths hung lax and ugly. In a corner a young man and his wife quarreled loudly, their shouts revolting with curses. The girl with whom Burns had waltzed into the conservatory, ran into the room again, her face pale. She stood rigidly in the middle of the floor and screamed. She did it again, kept that up.

No one paid her any attention, except to cast annoyed glances. Presently she grew quiet, stared about her. She buried her face in her hands. Her bare, warm shoulders quivered with sobs.

A butler, resplendent in livery of maroon velvet, stopped at her elbow. She looked up startled, seized avidly upon a white packet on the tray he carried. Her face was turned toward Wentworth. It was warped, horrible. A normally pretty girl, she was deformed by the dope, by her craving for it. Her mouth gaped in greed; her eyes were glassy.

THE BLOODY SERPENT

GRACE PUYSTAN

CLAUDIUS MOBO

Wentworth strode toward her, snatched the packet. "Listen child…" he began.

The girl sprang upon him, nails clawing at his face. Wentworth dodged her, carried her into the conservatory. Burns was slumped, half-dazed on a white stone bench. He seemed asleep. His face twitched now and then, twitched like an animal's.

Wentworth held the girl's arms, gave her a portion of the packet of drugs so that she became quieter.

"Child, in Heaven's name!" he demanded. "How did you get like this?"

The girl peered at him uncertainly, then threw back her head and laughed. It was shrill and senseless. It made Wentworth's blood run cold, so bereft was it of any human touch. He waited patiently for her to quiet. The laughing lasted a long time. At last it ended abruptly.

"Everybody's doing it," she told him, peering bleary-eyed into his face. "Now that it's legal to drink, nobody wants to. There's no kick in it. You gotta thank Grace for starting a new fad though. Everybody is giving dope parties now; only it costs like hell. You gotta have dough."

She fell silent, still staring into his face.

"But where does she get the dope?" Wentworth wondered. "Do you call up a bootlegger or what?"

The girl grinned crazily, "Sure, that's it. Just call your old bootlegger. He handles it."

Abruptly she flung her bare arms about Wentworth's neck. They were hot. Her lips, biting his in an open-mouthed kiss, were hot, too. Her body clung to his. As suddenly as she had

SENATOR TARLETON BRAGG

TESS GOODLEIGH

MARCUS ATCOLEY

seized upon him, she tore free again, darted from the room. He heard her shrill screams. Shaking his head slowly, he turned and found Pelton Hobbs frowning at him.

WENTWORTH SMILED slightly, walked toward the middle-aged banker, taking out a cigarette.

"You don't smoke, if I recall, Pelton," he said.

"No," said the banker. He had perpetually worried gray eyes beneath neat gray and black hair. His face was lined. "No," he said heavily, "I don't smoke." He hunched his corpulent body about, rested the other shoulder against a pillar. "Looks to me, Wentworth, like you're a little old for flirtation with a child like that."

"It's the dope," Wentworth muttered, looking guiltily down at his cigarette. "Don't tell me you're taking it, too?" demanded Hobbs sharply.

"Aren't you?" Wentworth asked, apparently surprised.

Hobbs denied it shortly, turned his shoulders again against the doorway as if he could not find comfort. His weight seemed too much for tiny feet. Wentworth searched his profile. The man had the same corpulence of the man with whom he twice had fought, of the man Chief Hendricks had identified as Senator Tarleton Bragg. Was it possible he was here to see that Grace Puystan carried out his orders? Was it possible this man had disguised himself as Bragg for some furtive underworld purpose?

There had been reports that Hobbs' bank, even with inflation and the increased amounts of currency and silver in circulation, was not in the best of condition, that his personal fortune was curtailed enormously. Had this man with his admittedly wonderful capacity for organization turned his talents to gangdom?

Wentworth spotted Nita coming down winding dark stairs, her lovely maturity of form the more attractive by contrast with Grace Puystan's slimness in blue. He bowed before the two of them and for the moment they were isolated on the stair. Wentworth was smiling, but his eyes, meeting the younger girl's, were commanding.

"Who forced you to start these dope parties?" he demanded.

The girl's face went white. Her dark eyes became round. She looked frantically about.

"Who is the Bloody Serpent?" Wentworth asked sharply.

The girl let out a small moan. Her hand grasped the banister for support.

"If you won't talk to me," Wentworth said shortly, "I'll see if the police…."

"I can't tell you," the girl said quickly, her eyes darting from side to side. "I can't tell you. I don't know." She fumbled in the throat of her dress, tugged out a small bit of paper.

Wentworth caught at it eagerly. There were scrawled lines of writing, and in red, at its bottom, a Serpent was coiled. A sound of charging feet whirled him about.

A youth in business clothes that contrasted shoddily with the formal black and white of the other men, thrust savagely at a butler, sent him sprawling in his crimson velvet and sprang up the stairs. He aimed a blow at Wentworth.

WENTWORTH SLIPPED the paper into his pocket, caught the boy's arm and held it in powerful fingers. The boy writhed nearer until, chest to chest, they stared into each other's eyes. Dark hair straggled across the boy's forehead. His face was pale, his eyes angry.

"You lecher," he spat out. "You and the rest of your kind." He jerked his head toward the Puystan girl, who had shrunk back against the banister. "Grace, darling," he panted. "Come away from all this with me."

Wentworth smiled slightly, pushed the boy away at arm's length and released him. The youth had a resolute face, direct, frank eyes. Wentworth liked him instantly.

"I assure you," he said quietly, "I have no designs against your Grace."

"Throw him out!" The girl's voice, almost hysterical, bit sharply into the silence that had fallen. "Throw him out! How dare you, Randall, come charging in here like this, insulting my guests?" Grace Puystan stamped her foot, her cheeks flushed. "Get out! Throw him out!"

Wentworth turned toward her. "Really, Miss Puystan, you're being harsh with the boy," he said. "He means well."

The girl's feverish eyes startled him into silence. This was not the girl speaking; it was the narcotics she had taken. The violence was the violence of dope. As Wentworth stared at her, she sprang past him and ripped her nails into the boy's face.

He staggered back with a choked cry. The girl stood crouched forward, panting. For a long moment, blood oozing from the scratches on his face, the boy stood looking at her. Then he turned heavily away. The door closing behind him awoke hollow echoes, and a woman laughed shrilly.

Grace jerked up her head and looked all about. She grinned lopsidedly, her face dope-distorted, then began to wave her arms and shout. She ran out among the guests, threw her arms about the neck of a boy.

"On with the dance," she cried, laughing crazily, "Let joy be unrefined!"

Wentworth reached inside his pocket for the snake-signed note Grace had received. It was not there! He frowned, searched other pockets, looked carefully over the stair and the floor immediately below. The note had vanished.

Wentworth stared about him. Close at hand, Pelton Hobbs was peering at him fixedly. The banker turned his smooth, grayed head to Grace Puystan who clung to his arms with both hands. They both gazed back at Wentworth, then, seeing he had detected their observation, walked off into the conservatory. Wentworth's burning eyes followed the disappearing Hobbs.

CHAPTER 7
THE SERPENT STRIKES

WITH NITA'S hand upon his arm, he walked slowly down the stairs, and at their bottom almost collided with the heavy man whose bulging forehead previously had attracted Wentworth's attention.

"Quite exciting, isn't it?" he asked amiably. "My name is Mobo," he added. "Claudius Mobo I was christened for some ungodly reason. You're Wentworth, I'm told."

Wentworth bowed, introduced Nita. "Exciting is only the

beginning of it," he agreed with the man's first remark. "It's the pity of it that grips me, the suffering, the endless pain and grief being bred here tonight."

Mobo nodded his heavy head.

Nita laughed. "Dick, you will try to shoulder all the burdens of the world. If you men are going to be serious, I think I'll hunt more cheerful company."

"We'll stop being serious immediately," Mobo assured her, but Nita laughed, shook her chestnut curls and walked away.

Wentworth took out his cigarette case, offered one of his private Turkish blend to Mobo, snapped his lighter to flame. He studied the man's face, illuminated by the flare. It was strong, the eyes quick and intelligent, the mouth jovial but ruthless, as so often are those of the mighty of the world. The flame's shadows emphasized the knotted forehead.

"I grant you," said Mobo, breaths of smoke underlining every word, "that you and I believe narcotics bad for folks. But remember that before prohibition, there was the same sort of talk about liquor. It drove people mad, it made men beat their wives, it bred murders…. Did you know there is an organization called the Association for Repeal of the Harrison Anti-Narcotics Act?"

Wentworth frowned at the glowing tip of his cigarette.

"And they're saying," Mobo went on, "the same things the anti-prohibition crowd said. That you can't enforce the law, that it creates graft and crime, that it's an infringement on personal liberty. They want narcotics sold like liquor. They point out the revenue to be derived from taxing it."

"You seem quite well informed," Wentworth said, smiling slightly.

Mobo nodded his oversize head. "I am. You and I may be sitting in on one of the greatest sociological developments of the century," he said.

Wentworth glanced up, saw that Hobbs was moving toward the exit. "We'll have to get together some time," he said with a smile. "I think Miss van Sloan is signaling me. Would you mind…" He moved off with a bow.

"Hobbs is going to the Rhumbana," Nita whispered as Wentworth joined her. "Grace is to meet him there later with some others."

Wentworth nodded, stood chatting until Hobbs had gone, then left also with Nita. He handed her into the Lancia, but did not enter himself.

"So far," he said, "there has been no violence tonight. But I can't believe they'll hold off much longer. You must be in the clear if anything happens, so you can carry on. You know everything I do…."

Nita's hands were tight upon his arm. "Oh, Dick, let me go with you!"

Wentworth leaned through the window for a kiss. "Don't be silly, darling. I was just frightening you."

"Dick," said Nita sternly, "you're the most unconscionable liar."

Wentworth stepped back laughing. "Ram Singh," he called sharply, "On guard!" But his words were Hindustani and Nita

did not know that Wentworth was warning the Hindu to watch over her with his very life!

THE LIMOUSINE rolled away. Wentworth signaled a cab and sank back into the shadows, his brows furrowed in concentration. Was it possible that Hobbs had slipped that note with its bloody serpent seal from his pocket while he struggled with Randall Towers? Or had Grace Puystan done that?

There was no way of telling, but the fact that Hobbs was going to the Rhumbana night club was suspicious. For the Rhumbana was owned by the Big Mick Harrigan, whom Wentworth already had found to be involved deeply with the drug ring!

Wentworth determined to delay no longer. If the federal men were intimidated, their ranks depleted, the police were not. He would call on Kirkpatrick. There was need for speedy action, but there were more facets to the case than Wentworth could cover alone. And the Federal forces, half their men murdered, were intimidated.

So far, the gangsters had not struck at the police force of the city other than through petty bribery and the subtle corruption of the politicians which the racketeers always had contrived. Stanley Kirkpatrick, the Commissioner, would help. They were friends. Often they had made common cause against an enemy. And the need was never greater than now.

The excited shouting of a newsboy caught Wentworth's ear

and, half in dread, he stopped the cab. Had the Bloody Serpent struck some new and terrible blow? Wentworth signaled a boy, caught the paper from his hands. A three-inch headline struck out at him like a blow in the face.

KIRKPATRICK ACCUSED OF BRIBERY

Wentworth gasped. Kirkpatrick, Stanley Kirkpatrick, accused of bribery! It was ridiculous. Feverishly, he read further. The Commissioner's accuser was Harrigan! The gangster said that, arrested for selling liquor without a license, he had been told by Kirkpatrick that for five thousand dollars, the thing could be arranged. Wentworth cursed. It was silly, and yet Harrigan's affidavit was supported by two others, made out by reputable men! The Serpent's work was thorough.

The thin anger of Wentworth's lips ringed them in white. He knew what this meant. The Bloody Serpent had struck at Kirkpatrick. The gangs had outmaneuvered even the fore-armed Spider, had anticipated his next step and struck down the one man who could most strongly assist in his battle against the narcotic racketeers.

Wentworth's mouth flexed in a bitter smile. His eyes gleamed coldly. Once more the Spider must fight alone, Spider against the Serpent. The Spider could spin a strong web. Let the Serpent beware!

CHAPTER 8
"ON THE HOUSE"

A S THE taxi wove carelessly through traffic, Wentworth read swiftly through the news about Kirkpatrick. There was a pompous statement from Glastonbury that he would wipe out graft in the police department, if he had to suspend every man on the force and call in the militia. A low oath ground out between Wentworth's teeth. Glastonbury was playing directly into the hands of the Serpent gang. Such statements, such bland acceptance of graft among the incorruptible forces of the law—for incorruptible the vast majority of the police certainly were—would do more to damage its morale than any other single thing.

The cab came to a stop and Wentworth, alighting, strolled casually across the walk toward the flaming reds and ghastly greens of the Rhumbana's entrance lights, past a man in elaborate matador's garb who bowed him into the doorway. The walls were crazy as a nightmare of drugs, distorted lascivious figures of men and women in the antics of some perverted dance. The glare of the lights beat down like a physical depressant. From above came the throb and thump of a rhythm that dragged the soul back thousands of years, back to the deeps of the African jungle, to drums of human skin rubbed by frenzied hands....

Wentworth went without apparent haste or alertness up the stairway along a garishly painted wall where distorted faces made mock of passersby, left hat and cane at a check room and pushed through gates of wrought iron into a night club built in simulation of a Cuban *patio.*

Small tables with hooded lights were crowded beneath *pergolas* to which clung artificial vines that looked poisonous. In the center, the ceiling was higher and painted like a tropical sky. The moon was lop-sided and red. Below it upon a minute dance floor, couples, squeezed together, wriggled to the sensuous rhythms.

Across the half-dark room the orchestra was condensed on a slightly raised platform, men who varied from coal black to light brown, men from Cuba. The boy perched on the box-like *marimbula* had black hair as wavy as a girl's. His feet patted time as he plucked single vibrations, at once thin and deep, from the flat-toned points of his instrument.

Wentworth sat behind a white-painted pillar and ordered a *Daiquiri.* When it came presently, it was like syrup, undrinkable. But at tables about him, thronged now that the music had paused for a moment in its maddening beat, there was a subdued surging gayety.

Wentworth was irritated alike by the music and the senseless gayety about him. His keenest scrutiny of darkened corners failed to discover Hobbs, and he was on the point of making a more detailed search when a glimmer of white at the next table jerked his eyes that way.

The glimmer of white was a small folded packet placed with a waiter's flourishing bow before a woman. She snatched it up, sniffed avidly the white powder it contained. Dope!

Everywhere about the city, at the functions of society, at

underworld get-togethers, in night clubs, dope! Available from the nearest bootlegger by telephoning, handed out "on the house" in speakeasies, as formerly they had passed out drinks. Good God in Heaven! Was there no end to the machinations of these organized gangs and their distribution of the hell powders that maddened and tortured and killed?

THE SPIDER stared slowly about the room, and everywhere he saw the little white packs of dope or the effects of them. He saw, finally, Hobbs in a remote corner leaning intently across a table toward a woman who bore the unmistakable taint of Africa in her broad face and in the kinky hair that, like flame, towered above a blanched face.

Wentworth's eyes narrowed. Was that what had brought Hobbs to the Rhumbana, this woman and not Harrigan and his narcotics' gang? He stared fixedly, his eyes becoming more accustomed to the semi-darkness. He saw Hobbs spill the contents of a drug packet upon the back of his hand, sniff it expertly.

A slow smile crossed Wentworth's mouth. Hobbs might be a genius for organization, but doping that way he was, not the Bloody Serpent. A man who could command this hell would not himself partake of its lethal pleasures.

As he watched, a movement in the lights at the door caught his attention, and the suave Claudius Mobo entered with a crowd of the younger folk from the Puystan party. Grace herself, laughing, hair wild and dress disarranged, strutted in their midst with the bold self-display that the drugs promoted.

Wentworth waited until they were seated, then paid his score and unobtrusively walked to the door. There was nothing to be gained by waiting here amid this narcotic-bred madness. His eyes shone coldly. There was work for the Spider. He strolled, smoking, into the lobby and, with more guests arriving, slipped out without hat or cane. At the door he recognized the boy who had crashed the Puystan party, the boy Grace had called Randall.

Wentworth touched him on the arm. The boy drew back truculently. When he recognized Wentworth, his jaw shot out.

"I know, Randall," Wentworth said quietly, "but you won't accomplish anything that way."

The boy's words were whip-like. "I don't want advice from you. You're one of them, one of those fiends that sell dope."

Wentworth smiled. His eyes were direct and kindly, and before them the boy was presently abashed. "Well, you were at the party," he muttered.

"Listen, Randall," Wentworth began, "By the way, what is your full name?"

"Randall Towers."

"Very well, Towers," Wentworth went on. "I want to tell you something about Grace. She is in the power of a powerful gang of dope peddlers. She can never be free; she can never even listen to you, regardless of how much she wishes to, until that gang is smashed. I am working to do that. Will you help me?"

Randall Towers frowned up into Wentworth's face. Doubt and a desire to believe struggled in his frank eyes.

Wentworth's hand was out. For a moment the boy hesitated. Wentworth's face was completely serious. It was doubtful that the boy could help him, but if he persisted in his intrusion into the affairs of the girl, there was small doubt that he would be killed as a nuisance. And Wentworth had liked the boy at first sight. The hesitation left the boy's face. Jaw firm, he clasped Wentworth's hand in his own. "I'm with you… to the death sir."

"I hope not," Wentworth told him earnestly. "Now, listen, Towers. You know Claudius Mobo?"

"Do I?" growled the boy.

"Good," said Wentworth. "He's in there. When he comes out, follow, but be sure he doesn't see you. Let me know what you discover." He gave the boy his card and strode off into the darkness.

At a corner drug store, Wentworth phoned Ram Singh and within ten minutes after the Lancia arrived, a vastly different figure of a man sidled up the street toward the Rhumbana. It was a bent old man with black hair that hung lank below his ears. He wore a black hat slouched low over squinted eyes and a lined sallow face. A black cape draped awkwardly from his shoulders deformed by a hunched back.

It was the figure of Tito Caliepi, whom the Underworld knew and feared as the Spider!

WENTWORTH DID not enter the front door of the Rhumbana this time, but slipped into an alley beside the building, found a narrow door that a lock-pick from the kit beneath his arm soon opened and made his way up steep, elbow-wide stairs. At the head of the steps a narrow line of light showed beneath a door.

The Spider moved soundlessly to it, crouched and peered

74

through the keyhole. A man sat alone behind a desk. He was counting money, crisp new bills that made a tremendous pile. His face was gloating, a coarse but shrewd face beneath a forehead that wrinkled like a monkey's forehead on which bristling red hair grew within two inches of the bushy brows. The man's shoulders were wide and powerful. He was Harrigan, the Big Mick.

Wentworth's hand closed on the knob. He thrust open the door and stepped across the threshold, an automatic glinting in his right hand. Harrigan jerked up his monkey-frowning face, stared at Wentworth's cloaked figure with incredulous, pale eyes.

"I would not move, *Signor*, if I were you," Wentworth said slowly. "Eet would not be wise."

Harrigan leaned back in his chair.

"Well, of all the nerve!" he ejaculated. "You ornery hunch-backed old wop! Do you think you can get away with sticking up Big Mick Harrigan? Say, do you know who I am?"

He thumped his chest with clenched fingers.

"Keep your hand clear of that gun, *Signor*," said Wentworth softly. "I would not at all mind shooting you."

Something in the calm, unexcited voice, something deadly and cold in the accented syllables, froze Harrigan's hand within inches of the gun beneath his arm.

"That ees better," Wentworth told him gently. "Now place your hand upon the desk beside all that money."

The monkey-low brow frowned until the bristling red hair

was almost against bushy brows. Anger corded the neck of the Big Mick, but slowly he put his hand down upon the desk.

"You're no stick-up," he said heavily, forcing the words out hoarsely because of his wrath.

"No," said Wentworth.

"Then, who—who are you?" A slight anxiety crept into the gangster's voice.

Wentworth smiled slowly, and as his lips lifted, two long fangs—celluloid teeth—were bared, glittering white on each side of his mouth. A curse choked itself in Harrigan's throat. His clenched fist crackled money like dead leaves.

Slowly Wentworth's left hand slid beneath his cloak, came out with a tiny cigarette lighter that gleamed against his palm. He advanced to the desk with a single stride, pressed the lighter to the desk and stepped back. A low whine of terror like a mournful wind moaned from Harrigan's throat.

For upon the desk gleamed a spot of red, a spot of red with hairy legs, that seemed to wriggle threateningly, *the seal of the Spider!*

"God!" cried Harrigan. "Not that!"

Wentworth's fangs gleamed again. "Yes that, my calling card, will go *upon your forehead, Harrigan....*"

The color went from the Big Mick's florid face. His jaw trembled.

"—unless you talk." Wentworth raised the gun deliberately until its muzzle was pointed directly at Harrigan's forehead. "Who is the Bloody Serpent?"

Harrigan's eyes widened, but the trembling went out of his jaw. It set stubbornly.

"My time is short," Wentworth said softly. His gaze glinted like steel.

Harrigan leaned forward, his hands white knots on the desk. "Listen, Spider," he said, biting off words. "You're some guy and all that. You've killed a flock of cheap crooks, but this is once you've met your match. The Bloody Serpent will gobble you up like that!" He snapped his fingers. "I'd rather face you any day, than—"

Wentworth was thinking swiftly. The man was talking too much. Danger was here somewhere. His eyes, narrowed, searched the room. A picture hung behind Harrigan. In its lighted surface, Wentworth spotted movement behind him…. The door was opening. He spun about, as three men with guns sprang toward him.

"Kill him! Kill him!" shouted Harrigan. "It's the Spider!"

CHAPTER 9
THE SPIDER
PREPARES FOR WAR

A S THE three gangsters rushed, Wentworth sprang to meet them. He struck savagely with his clubbed pistol, slammed the first gangster back upon the other two. They tumbled in tangled confusion.

Quick as a preying spider, he sprang aside, sent a swift bullet to smash the automatic Harrigan had snatched from beneath his arm. The Big Mick reeled backward, gripping his wrist, his face distorted with fear, his mouth loose lipped. Half a dozen swift blows Wentworth struck downward at the men who struggled on the floor, then he and Harrigan were once more alone in the room. His henchmen were unconscious on the floor.

Wentworth bared the fangs at Harrigan, took slow, crouching steps toward him, gun ready in his hand. In the hall, footsteps pounded. Men, alarmed by the shot, beat on the door.

"Need help, Harrigan?" a muffled voice called.

"The outside door!" Harrigan shouted. "Block it up!"

He grinned mockingly at Wentworth, and the Spider realized grimly that the Bloody Serpent had indeed put new courage into the gangs. Men who a few months before would have shrunk from the mere mention of the Master of Men, now defied him face to face. Unarmed, Harrigan still dared to summon help in the face of the Spider's gun.

"I'm going now, Harrigan," said Wentworth softly. "But I'm coming back. And when I come back, you'll talk—or you'll pray for death a thousand times before you actually die."

As the Spider spoke, he moved nearer the red-headed gangster with his monkey wrinkled forehead, so that, even defying Wentworth, the man became frightened and shrank back until he touched the wall.

The Spider struck swiftly. His pistol thudded beneath Harrigan's ear. The man moaned and slid down the wall, pitched on his face.

Wentworth fired two shots into the air, discharged a third that extinguished the light.

"Help! Help!" He cried in an almost perfect imitation of Harrigan's voice. "Break in the door, I…."

He started a scream, cut it short and laughed—laughed with the flat, piercing mockery of the Spider the underworld had come to know and fear. He screamed once more in Harrigan's voice, fired his last shot. Outside the door was an instant of silence, then bedlam. Weight crashed against the door. It shivered.

Again came the impact of men's shoulders against the office door. With a cracking explosion it crashed inward. Men ducked aside, sent the slashing rays of a flashlight into the dark room. A body sprawled on the floor, a tumbled black cloak upon its shoulders, a slouch hat crazily awry upon its head.

With a roar of hate, the men charged upon the body on the floor, kicking it and beating it with fists and clubbed guns. Abruptly one man jerked erect and started striking at the others viciously.

"Lay off!" He shouted. "Lay off. It's not the Spider! It's Harrigan!"

"*Harrigan!*"

The man who had first straightened pointed downward. Blows had knocked aside the hat. The exposed hair was bristling red. It was the Big Mick they had been beating!

WENTWORTH, WHO had crouched in the shadows and merged with the flanks of the crowd of men as they pushed in, slipped quietly into the hall. From the darkness he peered at the startled gangsters. Then he threw back his head and once more sent the edgy, mocking laughter of the Spider through the hallway, through the room where amazed men crouched over the huddled body of their leader. It froze them in their tracks with shuddering super-stitious fear.

Wentworth fled lightly, slipping out into the night club as roaring hate heralded a new pursuit. Beneath the black cloak, he had worn his evening formal dress and, the lank-haired wig and celluloid fangs removed, the hunch-backed deformation of his stalwart shoulders gone, he was merely one of the guests. He strolled through the crowded dining room of the Rhumbana, moved casually out, presented a check for his cane and hat and walked past two men who watched him

He thrust so that the venomous cane tip struck Whitey squarely on the forehead.

narrowly with flat, hateful eyes. Harrigan's guards were looking for their leader's assailant, but why should they suspect a man who departed with hat and cane? The Spider had left his hat behind....

Ram Singh tooled the Lancia to the curb, and Wentworth climbed lightly in, picked up the speaking tube as the car rolled forward again.

"The home of Professor Brownlee," he said briefly, and sank back into the cushions as the powerful motor beneath the gleaming hood droned into smooth speed.

Wentworth lighted cigarette after cigarette, thinking. The newspaper that had heralded the framing of Kirkpatrick had revealed other things. An editorial cried out against the crime wave which appeared to be nation-wide. It had demanded Federal action, and had itemized the new outcroppings of criminality, hold-ups, kidnappings, the murders of police by drug-maddened criminals.

In Chicago, a bank robber had loosed a machine gun on a crowd and had killed eight men and women. Yes, the Underworld, fostered by the golden flow of narcotics, had gone beyond all bounds. Crooks were bolder than ever before. Not even the swift vengeance of the Spider struck fear to their hearts.

Clearly Wentworth saw the explanation behind the mounting toll of robbery and thuggery. The Bloody Serpent had organized the ranks of crookdom into one vast loathsome army ready to do his bidding in any nefarious undertaking.

Wentworth thumped a clenched fist upon his knee. It was up to the Spider, and he would act. The flow of drugs must be curbed; this Saturnalia of crime must be checked! That was why he was now speeding to see his friend, the man for whose sake Wentworth had first become the mysterious avenger. The old professor devoted his life now to assisting Wentworth in his crusades. He lent the mechanical genius, the chemical wizardry of years of experiment to the battle. And now Wentworth needed his help again.

RAM SINGH sent the Lancia through Yonkers' narrow streets, whirled on and presently halted beside the small white cottage of Professor Brownlee near Croton-on-Hudson. The mutter of the motor released a flood of white light from a dozen hidden batteries of lamps wired to electric ears. For a moment the lights blazed, then they shut off, the door flung wide and the small alert figure of the professor was silhouetted in the yellow oblong of light.

"Welcome to Brainfag," he called heartily. "I began to think you'd never visit me again."

Wentworth crossed swiftly to the professor, smiled into his pleasant, nearsighted eyes. A clay pipe was clenched tight in teeth that were white and even in a jovial mouth. The chin was hidden by a silver-streaked, pointed beard.

"What's your problem this time, son?" Brownlee asked.

Wentworth's mouth corners refused to yield to the pleasantness of this foolish little home with its paneled walls of pale yellow pine.

"The problem I bring you is simple," he said slowly. "I want a cane whose tip will tattoo the seal of the Spider when I thrust it against someone."

The professor nodded alertly, small eyes alight. Wentworth's mouth became a thin line.

"I want one of the tattoo needles to be attached to a hypodermic that will eject poison," he said curtly, "the poison of the Black Widow spider!"

The professor lifted his brows in surprise. "That won't kill," he said, puffing out more smoke. "Just make a man almighty sick."

Wentworth nodded curtly. "I know Professor Blair made the experiment of letting a Black Widow bite his finger. But here's the point, professor. The spider was able to inject only a small amount of poison. If you make the hypodermic large enough to inject, say, a quadruple dose...." *

Professor Brownlee jerked his head in a nod. "That would do it," he admitted, but he still eyed Wentworth curiously. The younger man answered with a wintry smile.

"You wonder that the Spider tortures his prey?" he asked, and the smile vanished, left his mouth grim and set. "The Underworld has gone beyond all bounds. Strong measures are

---

* AUTHOR'S NOTE: An Associated Press despatch reprinted from the *New York World Telegram* of November 16 best explains what the Spider referred to. I give it below—

University, Ala., Nov. 16—For many years arachnologists have wondered whether the "black widow" spider was poisonous to human beings.

Doctor Allan W. Blair, 33 year old associate professor of medicine at the University of Alabama here, says they are. For eighteen months the professor tried the insects on small animals. Dogs and cats were not affected.

necessary. The Underworld, every man of the Bloody Serpent's organization, must tremble with fear at the mere mention of the Spider. And torture, coupled with superstitious dread, is the only thing that will do it."

"I'll have the cane and venom for you by tomorrow night," Professor Brownlee promised, and Wentworth sped back to the city. He called on Kirkpatrick and told the suave, immaculate Police Commissioner that the dope gang was behind the charge of bribery lodged against him. Kirkpatrick's blue eyes were icy, but his manner was casual. He touched his pointed mustache.

"When you are ready to strike, Dick," he said, "would you let me know? I am, for the present, unconnected with the police." WENTWORTH SMILED, recognizing Kirkpatrick's implied pledge of secrecy. For years these two had matched wits in a macabre game of hide-and-seek. Kirkpatrick had warned that he would do his full duty against the Spider if he obtained evidence, but meanwhile… So Wentworth smiled and promised.

Guinea pigs were made sick. Rats and mice died. Dr. Blair determined to try it himself.

After the insect had been permitted to bite his little finger Dr. Blair said he felt a sharp pain in his hand, which later spread as far as his shoulder.

He thought the symptoms would end there, but a few moments later he was seized with violent abdominal cramps. His blood pressure sank rapidly and in extreme pain, he refused narcotics until his reactions had been registered on the cardiograph at the hospital.

Dr. Blair then went to bed and spent two days in intense suffering despite continued injections of opiates. He was back at home today, weak and pale.

From Kirkpatrick's office Wentworth went to a dial phone from which a call could not be traced, and got a world famous morning paper, *The Press*, on the wire.

When connected with the editor he spoke rapidly, using the Spider's flat, mocking voice. "Don't attempt to stall for time, Sanford," he said. "I have a message that I will confirm by messenger in a short while. I am the Spider. The Underworld has gotten beyond all bounds and I intend to put it in its place. I want you to print my statement that Whitey Maxwell must leave the country permanently or on Thursday night at eleven o'clock, if he will dare to meet me, I will kill him at the Rhumbana, Harrigan's nightclub.

"Got that? Thursday night, that's tomorrow, at eleven o'clock at the Rhumbana…. After him, there will be others. How will you know this is not just a joke? My dear Sanford, I promised you confirmation by messenger. Yes, I know Whitey is good with his guns. He has killed five men to my definite knowledge. Good night."

At a corner drug store he purchased stationery and envelopes and in the middle of a folder of paper printed the seal of the Spider. Its wicked, hairy legs seemed alive on the sheet. Wentworth gave the envelope to Ram Singh.

"See that this is delivered to Sanford at *The Press*, but don't be seen leaving it," he said. "I'll take the car. I'm flying to Washington, and will be back tomorrow afternoon."

The Hindu bowed, cupped hands to his forehead, eyes glinting.

"*Han, sahib!*" he exclaimed and was gone.

Wentworth sent the Lancia swiftly southward, through the Holland tubes, out Jersey's super highway to the Newark airport, where he chartered a plane that sped him to Washington.

IT WAS nearly three o'clock in the morning when, a block from Senator Tarleton Bragg's old-fashioned home, Wentworth paid off the taxi driver who had brought him from the air field.

He mounted openly to the porch of Bragg's home with a free-swinging stride that yet was soundless. He unfastened the door with a lock pick with scarcely more hesitation than a moment's fumbling with keys might cause. As he entered, silently as the shadows of the hall, he slipped into place the black mask of the Spider.

Wentworth was positive the man he had seen in New York, the man he had heard threaten horrible death to a narcotic agent, was Senator Bragg, or a man his exact double. He wanted to catch that man off guard, to see if he could surprise or frighten information from him.

Wentworth stole up the broad carpeted stairs, found the Senator's room. He switched on the light and perched on the footboard of Bragg's bed, mask over his face, gun on his knees.

Bragg, with the light in his eyes, began to toss in the bed. A weighty florid man, he slept with his mouth open, his usually well-ordered white hair wiry and unkempt. His appearance was identical with that of the man in the white muffler.

"Wake up, Senator Bragg," said Wentworth conversationally.

The tossing stopped. The man lay flat on his back, and his mouth shut.

"Come, come, Senator Bragg," said Wentworth. "No fair playing 'possum."

The senator opened his eyes slowly, stared up at the masked figure of a man seated calmly on the footboard of his bed. He thrust himself erect.

"W-who? What?"

Wentworth leaned forward and pushed the automatic against his chest, and Bragg flopped back in bed.

"I come from the Bloody Serpent," said Wentworth slowly.

Bragg rubbed his eyes, shook his head and blinked twice. He went through all the motions of a man just awakened from a deep sleep and unable to believe what his eyes reveal.

"You're awake now, Bragg," Wentworth snapped. "You did a lousy job of that murder frame-up in New York, and I've been sent to tell you to do better or else…."

Bragg stopped his eye-rubbing, stared directly at Wentworth.

"Either you're mad or I am," he said shortly. "What the hell are you talking, about?"

Wentworth leaned forward, frowning. "As if you didn't know!"

"My dear fellow…" Bragg began.

"Cut that!"

"But, really…."

"Either you talk here," Wentworth told him shortly, "or I'll take you where you'll have to talk—the lime pit!"

The man's eyes were completely puzzled. Either he actually didn't know what Wentworth meant or was a clever actor.

"This is your last warning," said Wentworth, leveling the

pistol. "I would advise you to make your excuses and make them at once."

The blood drained from the Senator's face. His eyes seemed unable to shift from that threatening pistol, but he shook his head hurriedly. "I don't know what you're talking about."

"Hands up!" a woman's sharp voice snapped behind Wentworth.

CHAPTER 10
THE SPIDER'S FANGS

WENTWORTH DID not move at the woman's challenge. "My pistol is pointed directly at Senator Bragg's head," he said quietly. "Even if you shoot me, I can still pull the trigger."

"Not if I put this bullet through your skull," said the voice calmly, a voice Wentworth recognized. "I'm going to do just that if you don't raise your hands…."

"Come, come, Tess," Wentworth said pleasantly. "Why be like that? I was sent to find why the old boy here did such a poor job, and you…."

"I'm going to count three," said Tess Goodleigh, for it was the gang girl from New York, the girl who had been privy to the murder of Alice Cashew. "Just three," she went on, "and if your hands aren't up then…."

"Shoot him, Tess," rasped Senator Bragg. "Don't waste a moment. The man is dangerous."

"One!!

"Shoot, Tess, shoot!"

Wentworth voice was sharp. "If you shoot me, Tess, you'll have to answer—"

"*Two!*"

"—to the *Bloody Serpent!*"

A gasp behind him. Wentworth somersaulted backward at the sound, landed on his feet and whirled. The girl's gun hand flung up, but her moment's surprise had beaten her. Before she could fire, Wentworth seized her wrist and wrenched the weapon away. The girl sprang at him frantically. Her blonde hair was about her shoulders, half bare in a low-cut nightgown of silk.

"Quick," she panted out. "Hit him!"

Wentworth caught her from her feet, pivoted and stood her between himself and Bragg who was stumbling from bed. But instead of attacking, the Senator grabbed a telephone, shouted a call to police.

Without warning, Wentworth thrust the girl reeling into Bragg so that both sprawled upon the bed. In a single leap, he reached the light button and in darkness sped down the hall, sprang lightly from a window to the ground. Police radio scout cars, whining by minutes later, saw nothing suspicious in a brisk striding man obviously seeking a taxi.

THE CAB, found ultimately, took him to the home of Chief Hendricks, who came to the door in belted robe and slippers. Wentworth told him swiftly that Tess Goodleigh was at the home of Senator Bragg, revealed what part she had played in New York.

"If we can't arrest Bragg and haul him over the coals," said Wentworth, "let's work on the girl."

Hendricks frowned at him, massaged his heavy, unshaven jowls. His hair was tousled.

"Damn it, man," he said, "Tess Goodleigh has been Bragg's secretary for two years. If she's his mistress, too, I can't do anything about that. What has she done to warrant arrest?"

"She was on the scene of the murder!" Wentworth pounded out. "She was heard to say things which indicated she was involved in it."

The Chief shook his head, ran fingers through his tousled hair.

"Who's going to accuse her?" he asked.

Wentworth frowned. "I got a letter from the man who calls himself the Spider. He accused her."

Chief Hendricks shook his head. "You know we can't act on that kind of information."

Wentworth looked at Hendricks with narrowed eyes. "Getting scared, Jim?"

The aggressive jaw of the Chief shot out. "You know damned well I'm not. If there was anything at all to act on, I'd do it. But Senators aren't like pickpockets. You can't haul them on the carpet, or their secretaries either, every time you suspect them."

Wentworth's mouth became a thin, hard-pressed line. "All right. Will you have them watched?"

"Certainly."

"Grayson able to talk yet?"

"No," Hendricks frowned. "He's still unconscious, a fractured skull. I've got three men watching him night and day to see no new attempt is made to kill him." He peered directly at Wentworth. "It was Tess Goodleigh phoned us that Grayson had been kidnapped. We were looking for him when police got a call that apparently was from the Spider's taxi driver."

Wentworth's gaze was frankly incredulous. "Damn it, man," he snapped. He was on the point of blurting out that it was Tess Goodleigh who had betrayed Grayson into the hands of the kidnapers, that she had pointed him out to the men on the sidewalk before the Treasury Annex. He caught himself in time, found Chief Hendricks' eyes on him curiously.

"Let it go," said Wentworth. "If you're watching her, that's apparently all we can do. You'll let me know, Jim, the minute you get anything from Grayson or from following these other two?"

"Okay, Dick," Hendricks agreed.

BACK TO New York Wentworth flew, set Ram Singh upon a task and himself retired to a laboratory in his luxurious penthouse on Fifth Avenue, where throughout the weary hours of the day and into the night, he labored over a mask of steel that would cover his entire head and face. To the top of that mask he affixed the lank long hair of Tito Caliepi, the Spider's one recognized identity. Upon its visor he painted the face of Tito Caliepi—and the gleaming fangs of the Spider.

It was seven o'clock before Ram Singh phoned and reported, "It is accomplished, *Sahib!*"

It was eight o'clock when Professor Brownlee arrived with

the cane Wentworth had requested. The professor's old face was weary, his silvered beard bedraggled.

"You must sleep here," Wentworth told him and the professor agreed with a nod, glancing curiously but without question at the work upon Wentworth's bench.

"Have you seen the papers?" he asked. Even his voice was fatigued.

Wentworth shook his head slowly, pressing on with his work. "What have the gangs done now?" he asked.

"The police commissioner of Chicago was taken for a ride," said the professor slowly. "There were sixteen murders in New York yesterday. The papers don't even print separate stories anymore, just run lists of casualties as if this were another world war. So many robberies last night with this much loot, so many persons killed by drug-crazed men and women, so many girls assaulted…" his voice trailed off.

"It is a war," said Wentworth coldly, "a war that is the more horrible because it destroys souls as well as bodies."

Wentworth's face was gaunt with weariness, with the horror of these revelations. He bent more assiduously over his task.

"Tonight, God being willing," he said grimly. "I'll strike a blow at all that, strike a blow that will bring me closer to the Bloody Serpent…. But you are tired, Professor, have Jenkyns fix you up. I'll see you later on."

At nine o'clock, Wentworth was satisfied with the mask and dressing rapidly, sped to the address Ram Singh had given him. He carried the mask, the cape and coat of the Spider in a paper-wrapped bundle beneath his arm. The envenomed cane fitted into his trouser leg. He left the cab a half block from the address and climbed ill-smelling stairs to knock at a door that ghastly light only half revealed.

Ram Singh opened the door. Without a word Wentworth sat down with his back to a man who lay bound and in a stupor upon a bed, a man with a brown face and wavy hair—the *marimbula* player of the Rhumbana's orchestra! Within ten minutes Wentworth had been transformed by Ram Singh's skillful fingers—Wentworth had trained the Hindu himself—into an exact double of the man on the bed. Then, with a word to Ram Singh, Wentworth hastened from the building and made his way to the Rhumbana.

IT WAS nearing eleven o'clock when he arrived. The manager, cursing, met him on the stairs. Wentworth thrust out his lips sullenly and, at the manager's orders, slipped into his place in the orchestra, another man making way for him silently. The musicians were in the midst of a swaying rhythm. Wentworth's hands dropped to the keys of the box upon which he sat—the *marimbula* was simplicity itself to play, and he once had experimented with one in Havana. His feet tapped rhythm; his hands plucked out thin, vibrating sound.

Swiftly his eyes circled the place. There beside the dance floor sat Whitey Maxwell, the smooth hair which had given him his name shinily pomaded. Two women were with him and about the walls, Wentworth spotted men who were unmistakably gunmen, waiting with loaded pistols for the Spider to appear.

There was a nervous tension over the entire cabaret, which was crowded to its doors. The papers had been screaming with the sensation all day. Wentworth spotted faces that he recognized. Claudius Hobo was at a table against the far wall with Grace Puystan and others. He caught a glimpse of Harrigan's low, wrinkled forehead over by the wrought iron gates. Blue-coated police were on hand too. They wanted the Spider for many murders and the gangsters were willing that they should help.

The pianist finished the number with a thumping minor and walked around the grand's end.

"It's 'leben," he whispered, "or 'twill be in just a minute. When it's 'leben, I'll hit a chord and we'll all play 'Who's Afraid of de Big Bad Wolf."

He flashed his white teeth in a broad smile. The gourd rattler threw back his head in *hyah-hyahing* laughter that he stilled instantly. The pianist went back to his bench. The gourd man turned toward Wentworth. "What's the matter you so late, boy?"

Wentworth shrugged his shoulders, continued his sullen pose. The pianist struck his chord and the orchestra moaned into action. *"Who's Afraid of the Big Bad Wolf, the Big Bad Wolf, the Big Bad Wolf?"*

Silence first, then nervous, uneasy laughter rippled over the house. Whitey Maxwell laughed loudest of all. He stood up, taking a bow. The electrician entered into the spirit of the thing. He snapped off all the lights, turned a spot on Maxwell, a white spot that made his hair glisten, that glinted on the gold teeth that bridged his entire upper jaw.

"Who's afraid of the big bad wolf, the big…" Whitey Maxwell, big voiced, was shouting the words now.

Then, mouth wide, he seemed to choke, fell back a step. For

into the spot with him had stepped a stooped, crouching figure with lank hair dropping beneath a black hat, a dark cloak draped about its stooped shoulders. White fangs gleamed in a horrid, sharp-toothed mouth. Whitey's face worked, his lips met and parted like a fish gasping out of water, then sound poured from him, two words:

"The Spider!"

SCREAMS RIPPED out of the darkness, women crying out in fright, men shouting.

Wentworth raised his left hand, and, magically, silence fell.

"I 've warned thees man to leave the countree," he said in his thickly accented voice. "He refused. For thees, he dies!"

Wentworth raised a cane that he held in his right hand, raised it so that its tip pointed straight toward the gangster's face.

"Let him have it!" a man's voice roared from the darkness. "Quick, shoot!"

Guns blazed. Whitey snapped out his rod. Wentworth swayed, buffeted by the battering impact of the lead. But his right arm was steady. He thrust so that the cane's tip struck Whitey squarely on the forehead. More lead blasted from the darkness. Wentworth's head snapped backward as a bullet struck squarely on his forehead. He reeled from the spotlight into blackness.

But Whitey was screaming, screaming horribly with his hands clenched over his face. He spun squarely into the spotlight and for an instant his white face was turned upward into it. His hands dragged away, and screams burst out again among the crowd. For upon Whitey's forehead there gleamed a small, red, hairy-legged thing that was a scarlet spider. The Spider had branded his victim!

"Lights!" A hoarse voice in the dark was howling. "Lights!"

"Play, damn you, play!" a man barked at the orchestra, stopped in mid-note by the magical appearance of the Spider.

The lights flashed up. Whitey still stood swaying on his feet, but now a horrible change was taking place in his branded face. It was swelling with unbelievable speed. His entire countenance was a dark, congested red that was rapidly deepening in shade. He doubled over, arms clasped against his belly in an agony of pain. He cried out hoarsely.

Wentworth sat upon the *marimbula*, plucking its keys as the orchestra swung into frenzied action. His breath came in gasps. His ribs ached from the tearing rip of bullets that had pounded against his steel vest. On his forehead was an angry welt where lead had dented the steel mask of the Spider. But nowhere was there any trace of cloak or hat or cane or mask. He had thrust them down behind the raised platform on which they played.

And Wentworth played on endlessly, while the manager sought in vain to calm the crowd. Men and women poured from the place. Wentworth saw Mobo, frowning that massive brow of his, leave with Grace Puystan. Harrigan had already disappeared, and Whitey, convulsed and helpless from the stabbing pain of the poison, was carried bodily from the place. Police questioned everyone. Wentworth was no more sullen than the other frightened musicians and, after awhile, they were permitted to go.

Wentworth carried the deadly cane away in his trouser leg,

but left the rest of his paraphernalia. In a subway wash room where he hurriedly removed his disguise and, a half hour later, walked calmly into the door of his apartment building.

Under his arm he carried a newspaper whose wet black headlines shouted:

SPIDER KEEPS WORD; MAXWELL STRUCK DOWN

THE STORIES explained that Whitey Maxwell actually had been poisoned by the bite of a spider, that the brand of the Spider was on his forehead, and that he was a doomed man for the doctors knew no antidote for the venom that burned in his veins.

Two newspapers acclaimed the Spider's act in front page editorials, sounded ringing warnings to other criminals to flee the city, lest they, too, be struck low by the fangs of the Spider.

Columns and columns of history of the Spider, tabulations of his kills, of his major accomplishments showed the intense preparation the papers had made. The press had done its part in the Spider's attempt to brace the police, to terrify the underworld. But the news showed also that crimes of horror and violence were mounting hourly. The overnight list of murders, robberies and attacks on girls filled two columns set in agate.

Scanning the columns, Wentworth looked up to find he had reached his floor and that the elevator boy was grinning at him.

"Some guy, this Spider, eh, Mr. Wentworth?"

Wentworth nodded, smiling. The boy jerked open the door. And abruptly Wentworth hurled the operator flat on the floor, slammed the cage shut. A chattering burst of gunfire swept the hall. Lead bored through the door. Wentworth was bent almost double, gasping in agony. Bullets had pounded against his steel-guarded abdomen, beat a devil's tattoo upon his already sore sides.

Three floors down Wentworth stopped the car, darted out and raced upstairs, gun in hand. His face was grim as death. One story below his own, he checked and made a slow, silent advance. But the upper hall was empty. Instead of gangsters, he found a submachine gun masked behind a potted palm, its muzzle trained on the door of the elevator and its trigger rigged to start firing when that door was opened. Wentworth took up the weapon and, unlocking his apartment, carried it in. There was a tight, mirthless smile on his lips.

PROFESSOR BROWNLEE plunged almost into him, a revolver clenched in his hand and behind him bounded Ram Singh, long-bladed knife ready. Wentworth silently handed the machine gun to the Hindu, stood staring into Brownlee's narrowed eyes.

"It was a gun trap," he said quietly. "They worked fast. They must have been so sure of getting me at the Rhumbana tonight that they forewent to strike before. Now it will be war to the death." Professor Brownlee's jovial mouth was depressed at its corners.

"The warfare began yesterday," he said gloomily. "They wrecked my cottage and laboratory. I only escaped by taking refuge in that secret cellar you insisted I build beneath the house."

"Why didn't you tell me before?" Wentworth demanded.

Brownlee smiled slightly, "And what good would it have done?"

Wentworth shrugged. He felt suddenly very weary. An intense fatigue weighted his eyelids, and his bullet beaten sides ached.

"Ram Singh!" he called.

The Hindu appeared as instantly as a *djinn*, bowed.

"Han, sahib!"

"To the home of the *Missie Sahib, Ram Singh,*" Wentworth ordered. "Guard her with your life." He touched the hilt of the long-bladed knife which Ram Singh had thrust into the sash about his waist. *"It is war to the hilt, Ram Singh!"* he added in Hindustan.

The Hindu drew himself up proudly. He felt the honor that Wentworth bestowed upon him in setting him to guard Nita.

He bowed again. His *"Han Sahib!"* was a pledge. In a trice he was gone.

Wentworth strode to the wall, opened a panel and threw a switch. Across the outside door a panel of steel slid into place.

"That seals us in," Wentworth said. "Every door, every window now is locked with steel." He waved a hand wearily. "Go to sleep, Professor. I'll see the police when they come. Tomorrow I'd like you to make another such mask as I used tonight."

Professor Brownlee looked at him steadfastly, pulled his clay pipe out of his pocket and stuffed tobacco into it with a stubby thumb. "How about your sleeping, Dick? It's at least thirty-six hours since...."

Wentworth waved a hand impatiently, strode to the phone and told Nita that Ram Singh was on the way.

"Please, dear, be careful," she said. "If they know who you really are, there will be no hiding from them."

Wentworth laughed at her, made love to her, and extracted a promise that on the morrow she would take up her residence in his steel-guarded apartment.

"But you!" Nita exclaimed.

"I shall be gone when you arrive," he told her gravely. "From now on Richard Wentworth has disappeared. Only the Spider survives, and the Spider must spin a secret web."

CHAPTER 11
THE SERPENT RING

WHEN POLICE came, Wentworth assured them there was nothing they could do. The killers had vanished—*pouf!*—into thin air. The police were skeptical, but in the end they left, four of them together.

Ten minutes later, another solitary policeman, who bulged somewhat about the waist, sauntered from the building, twirling a night stick expertly. He cursed when he found the other men had left with the autos, and tramped off toward a subway. He went in through the exit gate and rode downtown. There he entered the washroom.

Five minutes later, you might have searched that washroom in vain for any trace of a policemen. He had vanished and in his place was Snuffer Dan Tewkes, his lax mouth quirked upward loosely at one corner in a smile. He snuffed loudly and, a bundle tied up in brown paper under his arm, slid with a half-furtive shuffle out onto the platform where the trains roared past, rode downtown and popped up on the surface.

He finished the night in a Bowery smoke joint. In the morning he hunted up a lodging house where a broad-beamed Irish woman rented him a room for three dollars a week. It had a single, dust-smeared window which gave on a low shed within easy reach of the ground.

As soon as he was left alone, Wentworth thoroughly oiled the sash cord pulleys until the window slid soundlessly in its groove. His next task was to do the same for the rollers of the bed, after which he carefully removed a section of the baseboard, fitted it with a spring that would hold it tightly in place, and placed within the cavity behind it, the equipment of the Spider, cloak and black hat and tool kit, and the cane with its venom-needle seal of the Spider.

Only when this had been done did he fling himself down on the mussy cot that, with a battered dresser and decrepit chair, made up the sole furnishings of the room.

It was late afternoon when he awoke and shambled out to supper, and in a surprisingly short time he came back with a newspaper and two magazines purchased from a second hand shop. He tossed these about, then, drawing the many-holed shade across the window and draping his coat across the door-knob to blind the keyhole, he sat before the distorted mirror, his make-up kit laid before him.

The wax came from the bridge of his nose. Heavy black eyebrows, shaggy and overhanging covered his normal, finely drawn brows. Over his head a lank, black wig draped its straight

He picked up hat and cane and without warning jabbed the ferrule beneath O'Tooley's chin.

unkempt hair. The grease-paint-covered tape that distorted his mouth was removed, his skin became sallow and dark, his nostrils distended by plugs of wax. A careful inspection and Wentworth was finished.

He rose, fixed a hair across the crack of the door so that he could tell if anyone entered in his absence, then went to the baseboard cupboard, draped over the dark tweeds he had donned a black cloak, drew a black hat over the lank hair and clenched the Spider's cane.

As he studied his reflection in the mirror, the Spider hunched one shoulder, crooked his back so that he seemed deformed—and extinguished the light. The window opened soundlessly. A shadow slid across the roof to the ground and vanished into the night.

ON AN elevated train clacking uptown, Wentworth was an old hunchback, hands clasped upon a cane. He picked up an abandoned newspaper from the seat. Headlines told him what he expected, that Maxwell had died in excruciating torture. They told him also that his trick of posing as a musician had been discovered. Wentworth read on, and his lips lifted in a tight smile. They had murdered the musician!

That was blind rage, Wentworth knew. They were frightened because Maxwell had died in torture. The Spider hoped his death would terrify the Underworld, halt its mad forays of crime. He thumbed on through the paper. The casualty lists in this fearful war ran to three columns of agate today, a stupendous commentary on the increasing thousands who were seduced by dope.

The tightness of Wentworth's mouth increased until his lips were straight and thin. Tonight, he would strike at the gang itself; tonight he would wrest from Harrigan the secret of the Bloody Serpent, or the venom and seal of the Spider would mark another man for the screaming headlines to record.

Wentworth got up and, leaning heavily on his cane, stumped out of the elevated train to the platform, turned westward. Over there the Rhumbana raised the stench of its destructive hell to the heavens. A dozen gunmen undoubtedly watched the place lest the Spider strike again. Yet he must go and as the Spider or last night's venture would have been in vain.

Wentworth did not hesitate. He entered an office building in the same block with the club, nodded amiably to the watchman. The man peered suspiciously and shoved forward a pencil-scrawled book for him to sign.

His eyes mocking, Wentworth wrote in a pinched, Italianate scrawl: *Ider Spay*, added an office number on the seventeenth floor and walked unhesitatingly into the elevator. The watchman still was not satisfied, but Wentworth seemed so utterly sure of himself, that the man's suspicions were allayed. He ran his passenger to the seventeenth, and Wentworth, nodding, stumped off to the number he had selected, slid his lockpick into the keyhole, and, while the watchman spied, walked bodily in, switching on the lights.

Behind him he heard the elevator door slam, heard the machinery whine as it dropped. He left the office, lights still burning, and walked downward until he was on a level with the tops of the neighboring five-story buildings. A moment to pick another lock, a silently raised window and the Spider was moving across the roofs toward the gun-bristling Rhumbana.

BUT WENTWORTH made no attempt to enter by the roof scuttle. He drew out the silken cord that was always part of his equipment, doubled it about a chimney and threw the loose ends downward. Snubbing the line about leg and arm, his cane thrust inside his coat, he lowered himself by slow stages.

He had calculated his position nicely and after three minutes of slow descent took an extra twist about his arm and halted beside a window. The shade was down, but did not fit closely at the sides and through a slit Wentworth made out Harrigan's broad back and bristling red hair. The indistinct rumble of his voice came through the glass.

Wentworth stepped lightly to the sill, peered through the glass. The latch was fastened. Clinging with one hand, he reached into his kit and drew out a small wax bottle of hydrofluoric acid. With its waxen plunger he drew a semicircle on the glass above the catch. Next he took out a small rubber suction cup which he pressed against the pane.

It was a work of moments for the powerful acid, such as is used in factories for etching designs upon glass, to eat through the window pane. Wentworth's suction cup pulled it silently outward and he was free to unlock the window. He did it without a sound, then crouched, listening.

"Damn it, Tess," Harrigan was rumbling. "I'm getting tired of all this stalling. You come across, or—"

"You'll do nothing, big boy," the girl chipped in, her voice brittle. "You'll do nothing, and like it!"

"Yeah?" Chair rollers squealed with sudden movement. His hoarse laughter grated. "I'll do nothing, eh? Well, baby—do you call—this—nothing?"

Wentworth's mouth opened in silent laughter. A gangster and a coy moll! The opportunity was perfect. Wentworth eased up the window, snapped the shade violently to its roller and stepped into the office. His gun was in its holster. The poised cane was his only weapon.

The flapping whir of the shade spun Harrigan around in a crouch, hand clawing toward his gun, his wrinkled, low, monkey forehead contorted in a frown.

"Keep your hand still, my dear Harrigan," said Wentworth mockingly, "or go ahead and shoot if you like. You saw last night that bullets can't harm me. Shoot, and then—" He made a stabbing thrust with the cane. Harrigan cursed and reeled backward, face white with fright. "... The sting of the Spider, Harrigan! Whitey Maxwell died, eh? But it took him twenty-four hours of hell to do it!"

HE FLICKED a glance toward Tess Goodleigh. The golden flame of her hair was showered about her shoulders. Her gown was red and close. Its silken highlights emphasized every curve of her taut, crouched body.

"Sit down, Tess," Wentworth ordered curtly, "and keep your mouth shut."

The girl ground out a curse. "If you'll give that piece of stuffed sausage what he's got coming to him, I'll *sew* my mouth shut."

"Sit down," Wentworth snapped again, and the girl obeyed. Her eyes were fixed hatefully on Harrigan's back.

The gangster had scarcely moved since Wentworth's swift entrance. Tess's small competent gun had been tossed to the desk. Wentworth did not bother to relieve him of the one beneath his arm. He raised the tip of his cane until it pointed between Harrigan's eyes, squarely at the narrow, wrinkled brows that drew bristling hair and eyebrows almost together.

"You know what happened to Whitey?" the Spider asked softly.

Harrigan's small eyes showed whites entirely around their pale blue pupils. His breathing became hoarse.

"Answer," said Wentworth gently, moving the cane forward an inch.

"Yes, my God, yes! Take that thing away!"

"The poison of the Spider," said Wentworth softly, "is in the tip of this cane. Suppose I let it kiss you gently on the forehead?"

"No!" Harrigan gasped.

Wentworth's eyes were pits of flame beneath the shaggy brows. His mouth bared those horrid celluloid fangs. "Yes," he said. "Yes, unless you answer tonight the question I asked you two nights ago. Who is the Bloody Serpent?"

Harrigan's head jerked in negative, frantically. The cane jabbed to within a half inch of his brow and he reeled backward, started to grab for the cane, snatched his hand away from it again in fright. Sweat started out in small beads upon his forehead.

"Who is the Bloody Serpent?" Wentworth repeated softly.

He could see the girl behind Harrigan, her eyes narrowed, hands clenched now in her lap. She made no move to interfere. Harrigan's chest rose and fell rapidly.

108

"I can't tell," he said with words so swift they tripped upon one another's heels. "I don't know. If I did, I couldn't tell. I'd be dead in two minutes."

"And if you don't tell," Wentworth said, smiling away his lips from the gleam of the inch-long fangs, "You'll be dead in twenty-four hours. And the twenty-four hours—won't be pleasant." He leaned forward slightly. "Must I ask again?"

"I don't know!" Harrigan's voice broke. "Before God, I don't know."

"He's telling the truth," Tess threw in from behind him, sitting tensely forward in her chair. "He doesn't know; none of them know."

"It's true, Spider," Harrigan spilled out words again. "It's true."

There was frightened sincerity in the man's tones, but Wentworth's menacing demeanor did not alter. The cane still hovered before Harrigan's eyes.

"You are a murderer, Harrigan," he said softly. "You thrust a knife into Alice Cashew's back. She had been your girl for months—a long time as molls go—and the knife was shoved upward from behind. Only a woman's lover with his arms about her could inflict that sort of wound. For that murder alone you deserve death a dozen times over, Harrigan." There was a merciless gleam in his eyes.

Harrigan dropped to his knees, arms lifted.

"I swear I don't know," he begged.

"You killed the musician I forced to give his place to me in the orchestra. For that also you deserve death, Harrigan." The voice was without emotion. It was like the ultimate judge pronouncing doom.

HARRIGAN'S ARMS fell. His head could not droop because of that cane which held his eyes like a snake.

"You have fed narcotics to the innocent who come here. You are one of the band of the Bloody Serpent that is distributing dope throughout the country. You are a party to the murder frame-up against Grace Puystan. For these reasons, I sentence you…" The cane crept forward.

"Don't kill him," Tess Goodleigh broke in. "Don't."

Harrigan was huddled as resignedly as a Chinese before a headsman's sword. The fight had gone out of him and there was only a vast fear. "I'll talk," he said dully, "but I don't know who the Bloody Serpent is."

"What do you know?"

"I know the man who ships me the dope," he said heavily. "Marcus O'Tooley. He came with a serpent, but I knew him anyway."

"Where is your serpent?"

Harrigan's eyes swung toward the safe against the wall.

"Open it," said Wentworth shortly, "and I'll suspend sentence."

"Don't open it," Tess broke in.

Wentworth flicked his eyes toward her. "I told you to keep your mouth shut."

"Don't do it," she said thinly again to Harrigan. "They'll kill you sure if you do. They can't prove the rest of this, but they can prove that."

Wentworth's left hand slid into his coat. "Keep quiet, Tess," he said again.

She took a lithe step forward, put a hand on Harrigan's shoulder. His head came up and he jerked his eyes from the cane for the first time, stared up into the girl's set face.

"I warned you," Wentworth said shortly. He whipped a tube like a cigarette holder to his lips. His cheeks puffed and Tess staggered backward, clapping a hand to her throat. Once more Wentworth's cheeks puffed, and Harrigan reeled to his feet with a hoarse cry, his arms thrust straight up. He stood like that.

Tess Goodleigh sank into the chair, her eyes glazing, her whole body relaxing.

"In an hour or two, you'll be all right," Wentworth assured her. "And this narcotic is non-habit forming."

Harrigan reeled toward the pistol on the desk, gasping horribly. His hands fumbled for it, slipped from the edge and he slumped to the floor. His breath continued hoarsely, slowly. The girl's eyes closed, her chin dropped on her breast.

Wentworth thrust the tube, another contrivance of Professor Brownlee, back into his pocket and crossed swiftly to the safe. He drew out another device, a small suction cup fitted with ear-pieces like a stethoscope. He attached it to the door of the safe just above the dial and crouching, thin silken gloves on his hands, began to spin the dial.

It took him three minutes to open the door. His swift fingers ran through the contents of the safe, but found nothing of interest except, in a small, hidden drawer, some packets of narcotics. They were folded as regularly as if by machinery and each bore a trade-mark name upon it.*

Some were "Snowballs" and some "Eskimo's Kiss." Wentworth whistled softly in amazement. The distribution of dope and its sale had reached the point where the gangsters dared to put brands upon their hell-powders! Probably they fetched a bigger price.

His mind rocking with the implications of his discovery, Wentworth probed more deeply into the compartment and touched something cold and smooth and spiral. With an exclamation of satisfaction, he drew it out. At last, he had the insignia of the gang! The countersign that would admit him to its secret places! Fires seemed to burn redly in his hand, a writhing serpent with its head reared to strike... serpent of ruby glass.

---

* AUTHOR'S NOTE: Truthful as I always knew Richard Wentworth to be about his adventures as the Spider, I was amazed at this revelation of his and inclined to scoff at it. But the other day I ran across a newspaper story that entirely confirmed it. I quote from this article, which appeared in the *New York World-Telegram* on January 9, 1934:

"Heroin packed in neat gilt boxes and wrapped in Cellophane under the trade mark 'White Horse' is being sold to the more particular class of drug addicts, Federal agents disclosed today as they exhibited evidence in the case of Bernard Tratner, 24, and Benjamin Forman, arrested last night on Fifth Avenue at 13th St., on charges of dope peddling.... The agents reported that Forman handed a package of 'White Horse' heroin to an agent, who passed $80 in marked money to Tratner in payment."

EAGERLY WENTWORTH thrust the talisman into his pocket. He straightened and saw the door knob turning slowly. He sprang to the window as the door flung open and a gangster with wide eyes and wider mouth stared down at the insensible Harrigan and the girl. He whirled and saw the cloaked figure of the Spider perched on the sill, snatched out his gun.

Wentworth sprang straight out into space, the silken cord twisted about his gloved hands. The man darted to the sill, thrust his head out. Wentworth, who had swung straight out into space like a pendulum, swished back, feet first. His heels struck the gunman on the chest, hurled him half across the room. The gun flew wide and he sprawled, unconscious, on the floor.

The blow checked the Spider's momentum and he paused on the sill, peered once swiftly about the room. A smile twisted his mouth, baring the pointed teeth, then slowly he eased downward through the night.

On the ground, Wentworth swiftly drew down the silk cord that the police called his web, balled it into a remarkably small compass and slipped off into the night, the cane tapping lightly as he turned from the alley back of the Rhumbana into the half-darkness of the streets.

At last he had the talisman. He had the name of one other member of the gang. He had spared Harrigan to the tender mercies of the Bloody Serpent. Marcus O'Tooley would talk, tell the ring's secrets or he would answer to the Spider. Marcus O'Tooley, chief of the shipping department.

Marcus O'Tooley. Wentworth knew his hangouts. He had

been a notorious rum runner, specializing in bringing stuff across the Canadian border in trucks. He owned a big uptown hotel where his henchmen swarmed with their women. It was a veritable armed fortress, but now Wentworth had a key. He touched the pocket that held the Bloody Serpent.

Uptown again, this time by taxi. He slid the celluloid fangs into his pocket, straightened the hunch from his shoulders, draped the black cloak across his arm, and swung the cane with a swaggering certainty as he strode into the lobby of the hotel. The black hat was jaunty over one eye.

He gestured with an insolent cane to a bellboy. "Marcus O'Tooley wants to see me," he said.

THE BELLBOY was bandy-legged, and his pillbox hat was as jaunty as Wentworth's black Stetson. He cocked a knowing eye upward.

"Yeah?"

"I am confident of it," said Wentworth.

His hand met that of the bellboy, who shot a suspicious eye downward at a corner of the green paper in his hand before he ducked a bow and became Wentworth's loyal servitor.

"I'll take you to him," the bellhop said, "but, mister, you're a stranger to me and I'm telling you that unless he sure enough wants to see you, it's going to be just too bad."

He led the way across the lobby, crowded with richly uphol-stered divans and chairs, rounded a corner to a small elevator beside which stood a sallow-faced man whose hands were sunk into his pockets.

The elevator was an express that stopped only on the top

floor. The door opened on a lounge even more luxuriously appointed than the one on the first floor. As Wentworth got off two men heaved up from a divan done in maroon velvet. They uttered no challenge, but stood with ready hands on pocket guns. Wentworth leaned on his cane.

"Could either of you gentlemen direct me to Marcus O'Tooley?" he asked gently.

"I'm him," grunted one of the two, a short, heavy-set man. His hands stayed in his pocket. Wentworth knew him to be Jake Lannoy, who had beaten at least three murder raps. He glanced about the lounge. Several other men sat smoking on chairs of gold and blue near a wide and heavy door in the room's opposite wall. They tossed their cigarettes to the oriental rugs that glowed with color on the floor. There were two girls whose sole duty seemed to be to pick up the cigarettes. They were clad like chorus girls.

Wentworth smiled at the short man who had said, "I'm him."

"Sorry to contradict you, Lannoy, and all that sort of thing," said Wentworth, "but you are not, as you so pungently phrase it, him."

The man frowned. "What's your racket?" he demanded.

"Narcotics," said Wentworth airily, "same as yours."

A snarl twisted the man's mouth. "I don't like the way you talk."

"That is mutual," said Wentworth. "Now be kind enough to conduct me to Marcus O'Tooley, or I shall be forced to hunt him up myself."

"Oh, you will, huh?"

Wentworth nodded gravely. "Quite," he murmured.

One of the short-skirted girls moved blithely toward them. She held her hands like a cloak model's, one up, one down with gracefully distended, and artificial, fingers. The nails were painted black.

"Mr. O'Tooley," she interrupted, "says show the gentleman in."

The men glared, then one grunted and jerked his head and Wentworth followed the short-skirted one up to the wide, heavy door.

Wentworth turned the knob and pushed in. The door clapped shut. Two hard knobs of iron dug into his sides. They were the muzzles of guns. Straight ahead Marcus O'Tooley, head of the shipping department, sat behind a desk. It was a bigger desk than Harrigan had used, but O'Tooley was not half so big a man. He had a small face that seemed chiefly devoted to sprouting a hair-line mustache. His entire countenance drew together to that point. His hands were clasped on the desk.

CHAPTER 12
THE SPIDER IS TRAPPED

O'TOOLEY, BOLT upright in his chair, said, "You wanted to see me, I believe?"

Wentworth nodded, glanced about. If the furnishings of the other room had been luxurious, these were celestial. The green carpet that completely covered the floor seemed ankle deep.

He took his cigarette case with deliberate movements from his pocket. He offered it to O'Tooley unopened.

The man's eyes met his curiously, then he pressed the catch and looked inside. He nodded, took a cigarette, closed the case and passed it back. Wentworth tucked one between his lips and lighted both.

"So what?" asked Marcus O'Tooley.

"So I'd like to have a little talk with you," said Wentworth.

"Go ahead."

Wentworth's lips tightened. "I'm glad to find you so careful," he said curtly. "I'm sure the Chief will appreciate it. Now kick these mugs out and we'll talk."

Marcus O'Tooley shook his head slowly. "Well talk as is. And you'll talk fast or you won't be able to talk at all."

Wentworth shrugged. "All right," he agreed shortly. "Here are orders. A new contact at Toronto. See Bertwin at 750 Carlisle."

"And what's wrong with my old contact?"

"I wasn't told."

"And why doesn't the information come in the usual way?"

The smile on Wentworth's lips was thin. "The Spider," he said succinctly.

O'Tooley started. His tongue tip touched his lips. "You mean there's a leak?"

"Precisely."

O'Tooley's eyes shot to the two men behind Wentworth. His right hand lifted an automatic that dwarfed it but which he appeared fully capable of operating. He pointed it at Wentworth.

"You two can go," he told his men and the guns eased away from Wentworth's sides. The door opened and closed.

"Sit down," said O'Tooley. "Where is this leak supposed to be?"

Wentworth turned his back on the gangster, pulled up a chair and laid his cane and hat upon the desk. The tip of the cane pointed toward O'Tooley.

"Either here-or in Harrigan's outfit," he said. "The truth is that the Chief isn't so worried about the leak as he is about you not turning over all the money...."

What!"

"—and he gave me that other message as an excuse to come here and keep an eye on you."

"Why, the dirty—" O'Tooley chopped off the words. "What do you figure to gain by spilling this? You know damned well if the Chief found out he'd—"

Wentworth nodded amiably, eyes chill. "And yet you're daring to knock off on him. I figure it is a good play to throw in with you."

O'Tooley stared directly into his eyes. "A good play, eh?"

"A good play."

A soft voice behind Wentworth broke into the dialogue, "As good as a play would be better phrasing don't you think, Spider?" WENTWORTH ROTATED his head slowly. Behind him stood *the man of the white muffler*, the Chief of the Bloody Serpent! The lower half of his face was hidden as before by white silk. On his left hand, held before him, was a twining scarlet serpent.

"Yes, my dear Mark," he went on, "this man is an impostor. He is the Spider. That serpent he showed you was stolen from Harrigan. Harrigan is dead now." His eyes smiled at Wentworth. "You might have saved me the trouble, my dear Spider...."

Wentworth smiled. "I'm glad you appreciate my poor efforts," he said calmly. He stood. "Well, I might as well be going." He picked up hat and stick and, without warning, jabbed the ferrule of the cane beneath O'Tooley's chin, striking him on the larynx. The gun dropped from the gangster's paralyzed fingers. His hands flew to his throat and he pitched over backward.

Wentworth sprang aside, whirled and lunged toward the Chief. His cane was poised. A single thrust and the seal of the Spider would glow on his forehead, the venom of the Spider would fill his veins. The Bloody Serpent's head would be lopped off. For Wentworth had not released the hypodermic needle of venom when he had thrust at O'Tooley.

But even while Wentworth plunged toward the man, the Chief stepped backward and the scene blacked out. Darkness was instantaneous and complete. Not a vagrant thread of illumination pinched in from outside, and the thick rug completely deadened all footfalls. No shot came from the blackness. Behind him Wentworth could hear the hoarse breathing of O'Tooley, partly recovered from the paralysis of that blow.

The Spider lowered himself to his knees and, cane thrust ahead of him, crawled toward the wall. His cane touched metallically. O'Tooley's gun blazed, but that was the sole response. A cool draft blew through the room for an instant, then stopped and Wentworth smothered a curse in his throat. The Chief had gone out by some secret door. Wentworth was trapped!

Wentworth sprang silently to the wide and heavy door, jammed into the crack of its opening the thin, saw-toothed wedge he had perfected for such use. He was not an instant too soon. Fists pounded at the heavy door. The sound was muted. Shouts filtered through like whispers.

"I'm coming for you, Mark," Wentworth called softly, covering his mouth with his hand to confuse its direction. "The Spider is coming for you, coming as he came for Whitey Maxwell."

He listened intently. No sound. The hoarsened breathing had quieted. Yet Wentworth was positive that O'Tooley still was in the room, that he was waiting, ready with that big gun in his fist.

"Did you read how Whitey died, Mark?" Wentworth continued, advancing toward the desk, but softening his voice as

Nita
Van Sloan

he neared so that he seemed to be standing still. "He died after twenty-four hours of horrible torture, twenty-four hours while the venom of the Spider ran like molten fire through his veins!" **WENTWORTH STOPPED** his advance, turned his back toward the desk and crouched, still talking. "I'll put the brand between your eyes, Mark, between your eyes. It will seem a little jab at first, just a prick of a needle. It doesn't hurt when a spider bites you. It's what comes later that hurts."

Wentworth sent his flat, taunting laughter into the darkness and fell abruptly silent. The battering on the door was louder now. The Chief must have directed the men to use a battering ram. Half-crouching, Wentworth caught his cane by its ferrule, swung its sweeping head in a slow arc before him. It touched nothing. He had hoped to lure O'Tooley toward the door. Apparently the trick had failed.

Wentworth took three long strides toward where he knew the window to be and, this time without masking his voice laughed. It was flat and mocking.

"Can't you find me, Mark?" he asked.

A curse ripped out in the darkness. A shot blazed. But the curse came first, and Wentworth was flat on the floor when the bullet whined past and buried its leaden death in the plaster wall. But now Wentworth knew that O'Tooley still crouched behind his desk. He laughed again.

"Do you think, Mark, my boy, that bullets can hurt the Spider?" he jeered. "Didn't you hear how Whitey—"

Once more the pistol blazed away, but Wentworth was masking his mouth with his hand now. And he had moved four paces to the left of where he had stood before. O'Tooley, too, had moved. He had angled toward the door.

Wentworth ceased talking and took four leaping strides toward the door, striking violently with his cane. It thudded on human flesh, jerked a curse from O'Tooley. Powder flame slashed almost in Wentworth's face. The explosion was deafening. Once more the cane whipped down violently, striking the hand that held the gun. There was the faint thump of its fall, and Wentworth was upon the gangster. As his hands closed upon the man's arm, the Spider laughed aloud.

"Retribution, Mark, my boy!"

A bony fist smashed into his face. Dropping his cane, Wentworth caught and twisted savagely on the wrist, wrung a moan of pain from the gangster. O'Tooley was small, but wiry as an ape, and he was half mad with terror. He tore loose and lashed at Wentworth again, then his arms were wrenched behind him, a bight of silken cord dug into his flesh and Wentworth found the light switch.

The illumination came from an overhead bowl, and it spilled softly into the room, onto the thick green carpet. Wentworth hurled O'Tooley from him so that the little man stumbled, tripped and, his hands tied behind him, pitched to the carpet. He bounced up instantly, but Wentworth had caught up his cane and O'Tooley's gun. He dropped the pistol into his pocket and walked slowly forward, the cane leveled before him like a sword.

"When I thrust you in the throat," he said, "I was saving my sting for the Chief. He got away. You can't."

O'Tooley turned and tried to run, but Wentworth still held the end of the silken cord bound about his wrists. He jerked and the gangster went down, shrieking with terror. Wentworth prodded the back of the gangster's neck with the ferrule of his cane, seemed to hesitate.

"No," he said, "I think it would be better on your forehead."

He rolled O'Tooley over, standing above him with the poised cane. Then he did a thing surprising in a man with the foresight of the Spider. He stood where O'Tooley could kick his legs out from under him! The gangster saw his chance. When Wentworth glanced up at an especially hard blow on the door, the bound man swung his feet and the Spider fell!

O'TOOLEY SPRANG to his feet, darted across the room, and darkness shut down as he kicked a certain spot in the rug. Wentworth, smiling, got to his knees. He felt the beginning of a draft and threw all his weight into a powerful yank on that silk cord that was fastened to O'Tooley's wrists.

A shrill cry tore from the gangster. Wentworth snatched a pencil flashlight from his pocket and sent its beam stabbing through the darkness. O'Tooley was sprawled on the floor, but only half his body showed. The other half was in a secret passageway whose panel door had jammed against his side! The Spider crossed to him in two bounds.

A smashing blow made the heavy door behind him shiver. The shouts came through more plainly now. As Wentworth reached the side of the squirming, helpless gangster, another blow smashed home, and light filtered through the door. Wentworth stepped across O'Tooley into a dark passageway, yanked the man to his feet and let the secret panel slide shut. He shone white light into his prisoner's eyes.

"Lead me out of here," he said quietly, "and I'll let you live until the Bloody Serpent pays you off for showing me the secret passageway. Refuse, and…."

Into the edge of the ray of light crept the ferrule of the cane, pointed for O'Tooley's forehead.

"No, no!" he cried. "No, not that!"

Beyond the panel, Wentworth heard the surprised cries of men. If the Chief actually was with them, he would reveal now the secret panel, he knew. He had guarded it previously because he thought the Spider securely trapped, but now....

"Quickly!" Wentworth ordered.

The cane touched O'Tooley's forehead.

"This way," the gangster gasped, and led the way twenty feet to a blank wall that opened to his skilled touch. Before Wentworth were stairs, leading downward, the fire stairs of the apartment. O'Tooley wrenched suddenly free. He doubled forward and butted the Spider in the stomach violently.

Wentworth's breath gasped out. He reeled backward.

"Here he is!" cried O'Tooley. "I've caught the Spider!"

He slammed toward Wentworth again, with his head bent; and the Spider, still struggling for breath, struck upward with the cane in his fist and caught him squarely on the forehead. O'Tooley jerked upright, reeled backward against the wall. Light filtering in from the fire stairs, glinted on a red smear on his forehead, a red smear that was *the seal of the Spider!*

Wentworth's mouth twisted in a thin smile. O'Tooley's violent attack had jarred loose the catch upon the hypodermic needle. He had branded himself, pumped the deadly venom into his veins. O'Tooley saw Wentworth's grin.

"My God!" he gasped, "not that! *Not the poison!*"

Wentworth jerked a nod, and a scream of pure terror bubbled in O'Tooley's throat. Shouts came from behind. "Where are you, Mark?"

THE SPIDER sprang to the stairs, raced downward. Behind him another scream tore out, then another and another.

Wentworth sprinted down two flights, whirled into the third. Gun flame spewed up at him, missed by a hair. Jack Lannoy, the killer, his short, thick-set body crouched, threw up his gun again. Before he could squeeze the trigger Wentworth stabbed his gun hand with the ferrule of his cane. The pistol flew. The venom was gone, but the tattoo needles would still work. They smeared a crimson seal upon the man's hand.

Lannoy whirled to run. Wentworth dived headlong, caught him in a flying headlock, carried him down half a flight of stairs with the leap. They brought up hard against the wall. The Spider yanked him to his feet. Lannoy was sobbing dryly. "You poisoned me! You poisoned me!"

Wentworth spat words at him. "There is an antidote for it. Take me out of here and you live. Fail, and you *find out how Whitey died!*"

Lannoy twisted around a distorted face, stared into the mocking eyes of the Spider.

"Death by the poison, or life, Lannoy?"

The gunman ground out an oath. "If I take you out, you won't let me die? You'll stop the poison?"

Wentworth jerked a nod.

"Come on," snapped the gangster.

He jerked around a corner to an elevator standing empty, the one he had used to come down. He threw the lever, sending the cage downward, eyes horribly fascinated by that crimson, hairy-legged brand upon his hand.

He reached the first floor, slid open the door. "Come on, fast!" he barked, and rushed for the exit. Men sprang up. A heavy man by the door darted toward them, grabbing for a gun, recognized Lannoy and hesitated.

"The Spider!" Wentworth yelled. "He went down a rope from a window!"

Lannoy hit the door with the flat of his hands. It slammed back and glass crashed. Wentworth pelted through on his heels. The heavy man with the gun turned with his mouth open, plunged after them. Around a corner Wentworth raced behind Lannoy. Taxis were parked there.

"Inside the cab," Wentworth snapped. Lannoy dived for it, Wentworth springing in beside the driver.

"Get going," Wentworth ordered. "A hundred dollars for you."

The driver saw the gun in Wentworth's hand and the cab jack-rabbited. The heavy man rounded the corner of the hotel. He yelled—street lights glinted on his gun. Lannoy, screeching, flung flat on the floor. Lead smashed the rear window of the cab.

Lead banged into the steel support by Wentworth's head and whistled away. More men surged around the corner. The man with the gun sprang to a taxi, throwing down again. Wentworth snapped a single shot backward. The hood's head wrenched aside. He spilled from the running board to the pavement at the feet of the other gangsters. They skittered to a halt like frightened horses and ducked for cover. Wentworth's cab whirled a corner. He turned coolly to the driver.

"Those men are gangsters," he said calmly. "I won't ask you to endanger yourself any further than the next subway station."

He took out a wallet and extracted a hundred dollar bill. "For your trouble," smiled Wentworth.

AT TIMES SQUARE, Wentworth phoned Kirkpatrick.

"Kirk," Wentworth said briefly, "the man that framed you and quite a few of his gang is at O'Tooley's hotel. If you can get some men you trust to strike quickly...."

"Right," snapped Kirkpatrick.

"Incidentally," said Wentworth softly. "The only important witness against you, Big Mick Harrigan, is dead."

He hung up and led Lannoy to a train for Queens. It roared beneath the river.

"How long we got?" Lannoy shouted in his ear. "How long before—"

Wentworth looked at his wrist watch. "About twenty minutes before the poison normally would begin to get dangerous," he said.

Lannoy's voice was so hoarse it was almost unintelligible. "For God's sake hurry. My heart hurts."

They got off at Woodside, where the trains ran on elevated tracks. Wentworth took Lannoy into a waiting room.

"When is the next shipment of dope coming in and how?" he demanded.

Lannoy stared at him, swallowed hard. "You promised," he said weakly.

"I did," Wentworth said, "and I shall fulfill that promise." He slid his hand into his vest pocket and brought out a small

128

vial, the wax bottle of hydrofluoric acid. Lannoy reached out for it and his hands trembled.

"You can never go back to the gang now," Wentworth told him. "I'll give you money to leave the country if you'll give me the information I want." He still held the vial in his own hands.

Lannoy twisted up his heavy-set head. "Gimme the dope," he said, pleadingly.

Once more Wentworth nodded. "It is against my principles to let vermin like you live," he said coldly. "You have killed wantonly."

Lannoy began to sweat. Beads of it popped out on his forehead.

"Nevertheless," Wentworth went on, "if you give me the information, I will give you money to leave the country. Without it, you will be tracked down and killed by your companions."

Casually he glanced at his watch. Lannoy's eyes glued on it, too.

"Okay," said Lannoy hoarsely. "Okay, now give me the stuff."

"When and where is the shipment coming in?" Wentworth demanded.

Lannoy licked his lips, eyes unwavering on the bottle. "It's coming through tomorrow night. A big truck with a trailer. Red truck. Company's name is Milo and Son. From Buffalo on the Albany road."

"Guarded?"

Lannoy's lips twitched into a grin in spite of his tension. "Just twenty men," he said, laconically. "Now gimme."

"One thing more," said Wentworth softly. "Who is the Bloody Serpent?"

Lannoy beat his hands against his forehead. "God! I knew it!" He took his hands down and his eyes were desperate. "Listen, Spider," he said, "that's one thing I can't tell you. I don't know. Nobody knows. He always wears that white muffler, and—in God's name, give me the stuff."

Wentworth studied his face narrowly, nodded, convinced the man was telling the truth. He handed over the bottle. Lannoy's hands shook. As he fumbled with the cork, Wentworth drew the tiny tube from his pocket and blew a narcotic dart against his throat. The gangster cried out hoarsely.

"You double-crossed me!"

He reeled backward until his shoulders struck the wall, slumped feebly down on a bench. He flung his arms about, but their action was undirected and without purpose. The bottle of acid smashed.

"You'll still be able to hear and understand me for a couple of minutes," Wentworth said. "Here's your money." He took a thousand dollars from his wallet and thrust it into the man's vest pocket. "The effects of that dart will wear off. And don't worry about the Spider venom. If you got any at all, it was no more than enough to make you sick. O'Tooley had already got the full charge."

CHAPTER 13
NITA IS KIDNAPPED

THE BRIGHT sunlight of May poking inquiring fingers into the mussy room where Wentworth had taken quarters, found Snuffer Dan Tewkes, the Cockney character he had assumed, sprawled half dressed upon the bed. It was twenty-four hours since he had abandoned his quarters for Nita's greater protection and fled here; forty-eight since he had struck down Whitey Maxwell to spread terror among the gangs; forty-eight since he had set Randall Towers upon the trail of Claudius Mobo.

The sunlight aroused Wentworth. He sprang erect, eyed in a mirror his day's growth of beard. He rubbed a tentative hand across but decided not to shave. It fitted too well with the character of Snuffer Dan. He left off tie, dragged on a gray, shapeless coat above mussy blue trousers and tugging a greasy cap across his eyes, slouched out blinking into the sunlight. The Spider? Who would look for the Spider in this guise? Hidden, he would spin his web.

He wandered up the street, plucked a newspaper from a trash can. The headlines shouted at him words that made his eyes narrow, that tugged his muscles to tenseness. He forced himself to relax and appear to read carelessly. For there was news that rivaled the newest vengeance of the Spider, news that transcended Kirkpatrick's attack on O'Tooley's hotel, though it was chronicled with the information that the Spider had struck down O'Tooley also with his envenomed sting.

The news that splashed across the front page was a bold raid on Tiffany's on Fifth Avenue, a raid that despite burglar alarms, special guards and the police force of Manhattan, had stripped one of the world's richest jewelry establishments of all its precious gems and metals! Machine guns, the newspaper reported, had held police at bay. Fifty citizens had been massacred. Only a few police had died. Attempts to halt the robbery had been feeble. The newspapers shouted to high heaven that the police were a flock of cowards, that they had made no very serious effort to check the looting.

WENTWORTH THREW the paper savagely down, forced himself to slouch into a Coffee Pot where, draped over a stool at a wooden counter, he drank chicoried coffee and munched doughnuts. Sliding a sleeve across his mouth, he pushed out into the sunshine again, shuffled across town until, leaving the Bowery behind, he shambled into a Fourth Avenue cigar store where he sidled into a telephone booth.

He called first Randall Towers, the youth he had set to follow Mobo. The boy's young voice was excited.

"Mr. Wentworth, that man Mobo is a crook," he shrilled. "And I think he's in love with Grace."

Wentworth permitted himself to smile.

"Why do you think he's a crook, Towers?"

"Well, he does such funny things, going to the Rhumbana all the time, and always following Grace around, and after police raided that hotel uptown yesterday, he went there."

Wentworth's eyes narrowed. "He went to the hotel *afterward?*"

"Yes, sir."

"And where was he at the time of the raid?"

"In his hotel room. I was watching."

Wentworth's eyes resumed their normal width and the smile was back on his lips. Easy enough for Mobo to have evaded Towers in his hotel, but Wentworth doubted if he would bother. "That's splendid work, Towers," he said. "Keep it up, but don't let him or Grace know that you're following him."

Wentworth depressed the receiver hook a moment, then called Kirkpatrick and told him of the gang's plan to run a truck carrying dope into the city that night. "Let's take it together," Wentworth suggested. "There'll be only twenty men guarding it…." His eyes crinkled with laughter. He unfolded his plan briefly, finished with, "All right, Kirk, see you at eight."

And then he called Nita, chatted gaily with her. "Don't go out under any circumstances," he warned, "and keep the steel doors shut. The gangsters are apt to be after me for last night's affair."

"And that of the night before," Nita laughed. "Oh, Dick, be very, very careful."

"I will, darling," he promised.

After giving some orders to Ram Singh, he ambled out of the booth, bought cigarettes, moved toward the door. His constantly alert gaze spotted a heavy sedan weaving at top speed down Fourth Avenue, slamming in and out through traffic. Wentworth spun toward the rear of the store, heard the sedan grind to a halt outside, and he dived to the protection of the counter.

MACHINE GUNS cut loose. Glass crashed. The clerk set

Wentworth tossed the vial. It struck squarely in the middle of the road, and blasted the night with red and white flame.

up a shrill, monotonous shouting. More bullets poured in. The front window and door were swept clean of glass. Lead smashed through the cigar cases, smacked a carton of cigarettes with a plucking sound, hammered into the wood of the counter. Wentworth, peering from behind cover, saw the sedan lurch forward, saw a heavy round missile tumble through the smashed window. Wentworth darted from hiding before the tumbling object had struck the floor. He knew what that was. He had seen—and used—hand grenades before this.

The grenade struck the floor with a metallic thwack and instantly Wentworth had snatched it up. He pivoted on his heel and flung it with swift precision at a high window that gave on the areaway behind the store. It smacked the window squarely in its center, crashed through. Before the glass had struck the sill, the grenade let go with fearful concussion. The window frame burst inward and crashed into the middle of the wrecked store. The wall bulged, subsided in a mound of broken brick and plaster, leaving a gaping hole that a car could have driven through.

For a moment after the bomb let go, the clerk was too startled to cry out, then he resumed his shrill screaming. Wentworth made the mound of crumpled brick in a bound, scrambled through the hole the bomb had made and raced across the areaway beyond. A basement stairs slanted downward and he took them in two strides, dodged a man pounding along a dark passageway and streaked upward into Third Avenue. He darted across the street, rounded a corner and slowed to a walk, doubled back to Third and mounted the stairs of the elevated station.

From there he phoned Nita. "The wires are tapped, dear," he told her. "They just made a try for me with machine guns and a bomb. For God's sake, be careful."

"I will, Dick. You…." Then, "It's come, Dick. It's come!" Nita spoke hurriedly.

The rumbling blast of an explosion vibrated harshly in the phone.

"They've blown in the door, Dick. Ram Singh…." The wire went dead with a ripping tear that told that the wires had been yanked loose.

Wentworth spun from the phone, raced down the stairs three at a time and slammed into a cab, throwing money at the driver. He shouted his Fifth Avenue address.

"Top speed!" he called. "I'll foot all expenses. And there's a hundred in it for you."

THE WIND whipped the final words from his mouth. The taxi bounded across Third Avenue, racing west. The driver palmed the horn and held it down. Traffic shrilled noises back at him but gave way. A cop on a horse whistled at them, reined into their path. The taxi bored in. He jumped his mount almost over a parked car. The cab flicked past the horse's tail. Into Fifth Avenue, the cab spun, skidding on dry tires, raced northward.

Radio cars were parked two deep at the curb in front of his apartment, six of them. A cop stood guard at the door. No use trying to pass him in this guise. Wentworth joined a curious crowd, sidled up to the doorman and asked questions.

"Geez, a gang of crooks," the doorman got out, "bombed their way into an apartment up yonder and carried off a girl."

"See the crooks?"

The doorman shook his head."I saw them go past fast, one of them carrying this girl. I starts after them and they shoots through the door." He nodded toward the shattered glass. "And I didn't have no gun. I called the cops."

Wentworth's mouth was a grim slit. "Anybody killed?" he asked slowly.

"Don't know yet," the boy said. "The gangsters slugged a couple of servants. May have cracked a skull."

Wentworth sidled away as the cop stared at him suspiciously. He phoned Kirkpatrick from a nearby cigar store.

"They got Nita," he said tersely. "They'll use her to threaten or trap me. I'll notify them through the papers how to get in touch with me. Tonight we'll try to take alive somebody who can lead us to them."

"Right," Kirkpatrick agreed curtly. "Dick, you ought to give up this work of yours. Someday you won't be able to rescue Nita, and—"

"You suppose I don't know that?" Wentworth's voice rose a notch. He forced himself to be calm. "Kirk, will you find out for me what happened to Ram Singh and Jenkyns and have them taken care of? Professor Brownlee apparently was out when they struck. See you at eight, Kirk."

CHAPTER 14
TWO AGAINST TWENTY!

DELIBERATELY THEN Wentworth prepared for the night. And when evening fell, in his own identity once more, he drove to the home of Stanley Kirkpatrick in a rented sedan. The two men shook hands warmly. Wentworth's face showed only pleasure at the meeting, disclosed none of his haunting anxiety.

Kirkpatrick glanced over the car, spotted a powerful search

light on the running board, a large radio loudspeaker in the tonneau. He peered at Wentworth.

"Are these your plans for the dope convey and twenty guards?" he demanded. Wentworth jerked his head in a nod. "Everything depends on tonight," he said. "I talked to Chief Hendricks at Washington today. That man Grayson who was shot will recover, but he knows nothing of value."

Soberly Wentworth sent the heavy sedan lunging through traffic, to the Albany Post Road. He recited slowly for Kirkpatrick the means of identification for the dope truck, red with the name of the company Milo and Son, which would be on its side.

"But we won't need that," Wentworth said. "There'll be at least three, probably four autos with it carrying the guards."

He drove to a stretch north of Tarrytown where the road narrowed and parked the car there. Fields of high grass were on either side. A hundred feet ahead the road dipped sharply, rose again to where a traffic light, alternately red and green, marked a cross road. Wentworth pointed the searchlight down the road, ran lengths of wire a hundred feet ahead of the car and into the grassy field. He touched a switch on a small black box he carried and the headlight poured a blue-white beam blindingly down the road. He touched-another and spoke quietly into the box. His voice boomed from the car a hundred feet away.

Then Wentworth walked back to the car and balanced a milk bottle on the fender of the car, a milk bottle full of dark brown liquid. He returned to Kirkpatrick.

"You take the other side of the road," he said. "If you have to shoot, don't let your better nature dominate. Shoot to kill!"

Kirkpatrick snorted, strode off across the road followed by Wentworth's laughter.

IT WAS a weary wait. Truck after truck labored up the rise just beyond where Wentworth had parked, tall trucks that seemed top-heavy on spindly understructure; massive ten-tonners with trailers decked out with lights of red and green like Christmas trees. Wentworth marked the passage of each under the distant traffic light with night glasses. Gradually the speeding hum of passenger cars became scarcer and the heavier drone of trucking increased. Then even those became few. It was far after midnight.

Two more hours dragged by before a passenger car that halted on a green traffic light caught Wentworth's eye. The roar of a truck engine beat the night, and a huge truck mounted the hill also. Green lights spotted its hulk. It lugged a trailer into view and both were red. The passenger car pulled ahead, loafing. The truck gained speed, picked up momentum for the next grade and two more passenger cars showed behind it. They made no effort to pass.

Wentworth, his lips lifted in a thin smile, put down his night glasses and picked up a small tube of liquid from the grass beside him. The passenger car spurted up the grade, paused as before at the top of the hill while the truck began again its grinding labor. Wentworth balanced the vial on his hand and waited.

The higher lights of the truck pushed their green gleam above the rise; its headlights showed. Wentworth tossed the vial. It struck squarely in the middle of the road and blasted the night wide open with red and white flame. Instantly Wentworth touched the switch and the searchlight thrust the blade of its brilliance through the night. Wentworth lifted the black box to his lips.

"That was a warning," he boomed, and his voice, magnified many times, bellowed from the loudspeaker in the car. "You are surrounded by nitroglycerin bombs that I can explode at a second's notice. That bottle on the fender is nitroglycerin. If it goes off, all the bombs will.

"Ready, Kirk?" he boomed.

"Ready!" shouted Kirkpatrick from the opposite side of the road.

Instantly a half dozen guns spat lead toward where he lay.

"Ready, Bill?" Wentworth boomed again.

He took the box from his mouth and yelled "Ready!"

Guns belched toward him. Bullets snipped grass all about. The two convoy cars behind the truck crowded its tail and joined the battle.

"Stop that!" Wentworth boomed again. "I've told you what to expect now. Do you surrender, or do you want to be blown sky-high with nitroglycerin?"

The two cars behind the truck jerked backward with roaring motors, took cover below the crest of the rise. The black shadow of a man sprang from one to the grass, crept toward Wentworth fifty yards away. The white light on the road made all his movements plain. The Spider lifted his revolver, held his coat over the muzzle to hide the flash and fired. The man screamed hoarsely and pitched to the ground.

"You men in the two cars behind, walk up the road with your hands in the air," he ordered through the loudspeaker.

Shouts of defiance answered. The first car blazed with fire-spitting guns, but Wentworth noticed with a thin smile that not a pistol was pointed toward the car with its dark exposed bottle on the fender. He drew another glass tube from his pocket, balanced it on his hand.

"This is the last warning," he barked into the mike. "Stop firing, or I'll blow you up!"

YELLS REPLIED, yells and more shooting. Wentworth knew they were covering the advance of the men from the cars behind. The hunched shoulders of three gangsters moved toward him through the grass. He lobbed the glass vial, flopped flat on the ground.

Once more a splitting detonation rocked the night. The first convoy car sprang into the air as if it had hit a foot high curb at sixty miles an hour. The nose, bathed in white and red flame, tilted high into the air, wavered and flopped the torn car over on its back. There were no more shots from it.

Wentworth turned toward the three men who crept on him. He saw their hunched shoulders halt, saw them huddle together.

"Surrender?" Wentworth demanded, bellowing through the mike. "The truck is next."

Instantly the doors of the truck flung open and men spilled out in mad panic flight, running down the road.

"Halt!" Wentworth ordered. They ran on. With a strong heave, he tossed another of the glass bombs. It struck well ahead of the men, hurled them flat upon the road. They did not move.

"You can't escape!" Wentworth shouted.

Below the crest of the rise the motors of the two cars roared again. They were beyond Wentworth's range. Impossible to bomb those cars. The gangsters would escape. He and Kirkpatrick had captured the load of dope, but the crooks themselves....

The three men who had been creeping on Wentworth sprang up and plunged frantically back toward the road. Wentworth raised his pistol calmly. He fired three times, and each shot plunged a man screaming to the earth. From below the crest of the hill, the motors still roared, but they did not fade into the distance. The crashing reports of pistols came as fast as machine gun detonations. Kirkpatrick! Single-handed, Kirkpatrick had engaged the gang cars containing at least ten men!

Wentworth sprang up and, circling the men he had dropped, crouched opposite the remaining two gang cars. He saw a truck stop at the top of the hill beneath the traffic light, saw it begin to turn back. He jerked his gaze back to the gang cars. He saw then, by the glare of their headlights, by the reflected brilliance of his searchlight, the reason the cars had not moved. The tires of both were punctured and as Wentworth watched the engines began to cough. One quit; the other backfired with a dying motor. Gasoline poured in glistening thin streams from their bullet-pierced tanks.

"Surrender!" Wentworth heard Kirkpatrick shout. "Surrender, or I'll blow you to hell!"

A renewed roll of gunfire answered him. Wentworth, crouching, considered. He had three more bombs in his pocket, but if he tossed one now, both stalled cars would be wrecked, all their occupants killed and he would have no man to tell him where the Chief of the Bloody Serpent had his lair. The glistening streams of gasoline died. The men remained closed tightly in their bulletproof cars, firing through narrow slits.

They could not escape, but neither could Wentworth and Kirkpatrick short of blowing up the cars, drive them out. A cold smile twitched Wentworth's lips. He turned his back on the still-fighting cars, crouched in the grass and, masking his face beneath his coat, lighted a cigarette. He puffed it to a bright coal, then turned and flipped it in a high arch toward the cars.

It struck the top of one, rolled backward, a tiny, glowing spot of red in the darkness. It toppled over the curved rear, struck the bumper and scattered burning sparks down upon the gasoline wet road! Immediately there was a burst of fire. Blue and white flames danced over the road bed, lapped the back of the cars. Men turned white, frightened faces that showed like pale ghosts in the flickering light.

A DOOR flung open on Wentworth's side, and a man sprang to the road, gun clenched in his hand.

"Surrender!" Wentworth shouted.

A shot answered, and Wentworth dropped the man in his tracks. Two more spilled from the opposite side, and Kirkpatrick's gun blasted twice, nailed them to the flaming roadway.

"Surrender!" Wentworth whooped.

A defiant jeer answered him. In a body, the remaining seven

men burst out and charged straight toward him, away from the devastating fire of Kirkpatrick. Three of the men fell before the charge plunged into the grass and the survivors threw themselves flat for cover. Only four were left, but those four crept toward Wentworth.

A bomb would wipe them out in one swoop, but a bomb would destroy all chance of gaining a clue to the leader. Wentworth smiled grimly, uncorked his vials and poured their contents on the earth, crept backward away from the spot and waited. Once more, guardedly, he lighted a cigarette.

From the blackness ahead, a shot sent lead questing for him. From the far side of the road, a gun roared and a gangster reeled to his feet with a cry of pain, flung down again woodenly and was silent. Three of them left now. A roaring motor jerked Wentworth's head to the left. Another traveler had stumbled on the battle scene and was fleeing. He would be certain to give the alarm from the first phone. Police would soon be on the way.

Wentworth retreated still farther, the cigarette in the hollow of his hand. He drew a blackjack and laid it ready in the grass before him; then, when he calculated that the three who converged on him had passed the point where he had slipped the explosives, once more he flipped a cigarette in a graceful accurate arch. A swish of explosive flame gushed upward.

Wentworth, crouching ready, saw three men jerk up in fright. He fired twice like lightning before the flame died and like lightning bolts his bullets sped, slamming two men into bloody death. Instantly he was up and dashing toward the third man.

Two yards from him, Wentworth sprang to one side, ducked, weaved back to the left. A shot spat flame almost into his face. The brim of his hat snapped upward, torn by the lead. Wentworth dived and lashed out with the blackjack, struck flesh that cried out in pain. A smashing blow of iron numbed Wentworth's left arm. He lunged forward, swinging again.

His leather swished emptily and he ducked under a second crushing blow from the gangster's gun. His dive flung him bodily against the man. He felt the prod of steel in his ribs, and reaching up behind the gunman, snapped the blackjack desperately against the back of his head. The man's skull slammed forward, struck Wentworth on the mouth painfully. The body relaxed in his arms.

Wentworth thrust him aside, sat up dizzily.

"All right, Kirk," he called, his voice thick. "I got one alive."

Not ten feet away a gun blasted, spitting flame toward him. Wentworth threw himself desperately aside. He snatched out his gun, but, with it raised, hesitated. The quick booming flash of that weapon had sounded familiar, the head that was outlined against the dimming glare of the gasoline… Good Lord, it was Kirkpatrick!

"What the hell's the matter with you, Kirk?" he demanded angrily, hugging the ground. "Have you gone insane?"

"You surrender, or the next bullet will bore your belly," Kirkpatrick growled. "You can't fool me!"

"Damn it, Kirk…."

Another bullet burned the air between them, skimming the top of the grass.

CHAPTER 15
THE DIM TRAIL

WENTWORTH GASPED at that second shot. He kicked the ground. His arms floundered in the soft grass for a few moments, then he was still. The gaunt, tall figure of Kirkpatrick straightened and moved cautiously toward where he lay. A gun glinted in the commissioner's hand, and he sent the white ray of a flashlight tearing through the darkness. He picked out the two inert bodies in the grass and inched nearer.

When he saw Wentworth, a great cry rose in his throat. He flung himself down beside him, jerked him over on his back.

"Dick, Dick! For God's sake, Dick. I didn't—"

Wentworth opened his eyes. "No, damn you," he mumbled with his battered lips. "You didn't, but it wasn't your fault. What the hell's the matter with you?"

Kirkpatrick laughed weakly. "I thought I saw you killed, saw you go up in smoke when those flames shot up a while ago. I thought a bullet had hit one of your bombs. I was so sure of it...."

Wentworth snatched Kirkpatrick's gun from his hand and fired almost pointblank at him. A man screamed and Kirkpatrick did a back-flip, struggling like a trapped lion.

"Quit wrestling that dead man around," Wentworth told him. "He had his gun ready to blow you out and I just got him in time."

Kirkpatrick threw off the weight angrily, turned and stared down into the face of the man he illuminated with his flashlight.

"After I went to all the trouble to capture that man alive," said Wentworth grimly, "I have to shoot him to save your worthless life. He reared up like a ghost behind you with that gun."

Kirkpatrick said "Thanks" heavily. He turned toward Wentworth. "I'm sorry as hell," he said. "I know how much capturing one of these men meant to you. I see now what was the matter. I was sure you were dead and your mouth is so swollen your voice didn't sound natural."

Wentworth thrust himself to his knees, "Put the light here," he said, and, favoring his injured arm, he searched the body of the gangster. There was nothing of interest on him, but finally, after a hurried search of the bodies of the other men who had died, he discovered in the charred clothes of a gangster who had fallen into the gasoline flames, a fragment of paper with a New York telephone number on it. And in the man's pocket, Wentworth found also the fragments of a Bloody Serpent ring. Evidently this was the leader of the convoy gang.

Dimly now from the distance, came the roar of racing motors. Wentworth jerked erect, stared into Kirkpatrick's eyes.

"You stay here, Kirk," said Wentworth, "and explain to the police about this thing. I've got to get to town."

Kirkpatrick frowned. "Damn it, you can't walk out on me like this!"

Wentworth smiled. "Can you imagine Richard Wentworth explaining to these nosey district attorneys how he got wind of this and…" he shrugged. "Don't forget that while there's no proof that this same Wentworth is the Spider, he's been accused of it often enough for his connection with any crime to become dangerous."

"But there's no seal here!"

Wentworth shook his head slowly, still smiling. "Not a seal," he said. He listened again. The roar of the motors was nearer. Wentworth clapped Kirkpatrick on the shoulder. "I'll be seeing you," he said, and ran, nursing his injured arm, toward the parked automobile that still spilled its brilliant light down the roadway.

Twenty dead men upon whom the Spider had placed no seal. Twenty dead for whom Kirkpatrick must take unwilling credit. But Wentworth had not brought his friend along on this expedition for the help he might give. His trap would have worked equally well single handed. And the Spider preferred to work alone. This was as he had intended it. Kirkpatrick tomorrow would be the hero of the city, of the entire country. Single-handed, he had captured a huge cargo of dope and killed twenty gangsters.

That would do much to lift the onus of the charge of bribery lodged against him. It would bring him the fulsome praise of newspapers. Most important of all, it would bring courage and hope to the ranks of the men he had led so well and so bravely, the police of New York.

WENTWORTH DROVE with careful speed into the northern limits of Manhattan before, parking near a drug store, he entered and phoned the "Who called me?" Service. When he had given the number he had found on the charred slip of the convoy leader's body, he waited with pounding heart. On his right temple the thin white scar throbbed red and violent.

Would this prove to be a clue, or would the Serpent once more have squirmed from his imprisoning hands. Would....

"Yes," he said eagerly. "No it can't be that."

It was almost a cry, his frantic protest. So much had hinged on this number, and now... "Very well," he said. "Thank you," and he hung up a receiver that weighed a ton in his hand, turned with dragging shoulders out of the booth. Abruptly he spun toward the telephone directory and located the name the operator had given opposite the number he had found. "Doctor's Exchange" it read, an office with which doctors listed their itineraries so that patients could locate them at any time.

Wentworth strode from the building and sped to the Doctor's Exchange.

A twenty dollar tip gained him access to the exchange books for three months back and he listed the new subscribers, forty-five of them. One of these, he was sure was the name behind which the Bloody Serpent masqueraded, but which one?

Wentworth's federal credentials opened the Board of Health offices, but there he learned only that all the men listed really were doctors.

The Department of Justice's private list of doctors suspected of illegal distribution of drugs gave him no help. Wentworth had one more chance. He had the department route out the credit secretary of the Retail Merchants' Bureau and let him search the files. There, he found that three doctors on the exchange list had paid off large debts in the last three months after falling far behind. One of these men had paid off two thousand dollars in a month. His name was Dr. Horace Skeen.

Eyes eagerly alight, Wentworth hurried back to the Doctor's Exchange and looked up Skeen. He found that, day or night, the doctor left only one phone number with the exchange. That number varied from one end of town to the other, but there was always only one. Wentworth traced the number given for that night and found it was a pay station in an all-night drug store. Smiling grimly, he called it and asked for Dr. Horace Skeen.

"The doctor just left," a man said, and gave Wentworth another number.

Three times Wentworth went through that process, and finally got a woman who said: "Give me your number and I'll have Dr. Skeen call you right back. I can't get him to the phone now."

Wentworth gave the number of the pay phone he was using, and added: "It's important!"

Within two minutes, the phone rang sharply and Wentworth lifted the receiver, heart thumping high in his throat. His hand, gripping the hard black rubber, was tense. Was he at last gaining a clue to the Bloody Serpent? Had he at last found a trail that would rescue Nita, wrest the world from the cruel threat of dope?

The voice over the wire was rasping. "This is a hell of a time to wake anybody up. What do you want?"

"Is this Dr. Skeen?" Wentworth demanded.

"Yes." The man bit off the word.

"They told me to call you up when I got here."

"All right," snapped the man, irritated. "Report."

"I just want to be sure…" Wentworth stalled.

The voice on the wire became soft and sibilant. "This once," it said with menace, "we will waive the formalities. Will you have the kindness to explain why you awakened me at this ungodly hour?"

"Okay, okay," said Wentworth, his voice distorted. "I just wanted to know it was you, Chief. Listen, somebody stuck up the truck and killed the whole bunch of us except just me."

"What!" The voice hurt Wentworth's ear.

"Yeah," said Wentworth fumblingly. "Every damned one except me."

"And they got the dope, too?" Fury trembled over the wire.

"Yeah. Like I'm telling you. It was like this…."

The voice became soft again. "I'd like you to report in person," it said. "Where are you? I'll send a car for you."

Wentworth's eyes narrowed on the phone. "Sure, Chief," he said. "I'm in a drug store at the corner of Ninety-sixt' and Broadway."

"Wait there," said the Chief and hung up.

WAIT? WENTWORTH laughed sharply. Wild horses could not pull him from the spot. Working swiftly in the booth while he put through a call for his own apartment, he transformed his features with makeup. He gave himself sunken eyes and bulbous nose, made his ears fan out from his head with a wedge of wax behind them and similarly made his lips protrude. Presently the quick voice of Professor Brownlee answered. Wentworth thrust aside inquiries, learned Ram Singh had been only stunned by the force of the explosion that had blown in the door and got him on the wire.

Then Wentworth switched immediately into Hindustani, giving swift, detailed instructions to the Hindu. Then he strode outside and found a taxi driver whom a fifty dollar bill made lend an attentive ear to his orders. These arrangements made, Wentworth, shoulders slouching now, hands deep in his pockets and head thrust forward in a belligerent pose, waited for the Chief.

Presently a heavy sedan rolled up to where he stood and a man called from the dark interior:

"You phoned Dr. Skeen?"

Wentworth nodded, stepped toward the car. Abruptly he flung aside, dropping to the street and rolling swiftly down the grade of 96th Street. The man, without warning, had jerked his hand above the edge of the door and opened fire with an automatic. The shots scorched the air where Wentworth had stood a moment before, scarred the pavement in swift pursuit. The Spider sprang to his feet, dived behind a car and jerked out a gun. But the sedan spurted and whirled the corner, unharmed.

Wentworth sprang to his cab and they spun around the corner in the wake of the Chief's car. For three miles they dodged, before the sedan, hitting open country, distanced the valiant but lower-powered taxi. Wentworth, eyes bitter with disappointment, gave his home address and there, disguise removed, stalked openly into the lobby.

Let the Bloody Serpent locate him! Let the gangsters come

153

in droves to expunge the Spider from the rolls of its enemies! Wentworth's fists clenched at his sides. By God, he was ready!

He strode flat-footed, angry, across the hall to his door, pushed in and Professor Brownlee bounced up from a divan to greet him. "I knew you were coming," he said. "I got your message."

Wentworth stopped short in his tracks. "What message?" he demanded.

"Why, a Dr. Skeen called and said you'd be right home," said Professor Brownlee, blinking his dark eyes in bewilderment. "He said you were to call him the moment you got in."

Dr. Skeen! Once more the keen-minded Chief of the Bloody Serpent had foreguessed his movements, once more had squirmed free of the Spider's carefully woven web. But at last they were at grips. At least Wentworth could communicate with the Chief, even though his hands were tied in advance by the gangster's capture of Nita. His mouth grim, Wentworth strode to the phone. Once more the old battle raged within his heart—his love for Nita against his duty to the ideals of the Spider.

Nita was the sacrifice, laid white and helpless upon the altar of his grim service to humanity. Nita, the sacrifice and the Spider the executioner! Slowly Wentworth gave the number of the Bloody Serpent to the operator.

"Just a moment," said the woman's voice, a voice that this time narrowed Wentworth's eyes grimly with recognition, the voice of Tess Goodleigh.

"The Spider calling, Tess," he drawled. "Tell the Chief I'm

at home—and receiving callers with open arms. Won't you come into my parlor?"

And he slammed up the receiver savagely.

PROFESSOR BROWNLEE stood in the doorway, watching Wentworth. The Spider took a swift turn up and down the floor, eyes scarcely swerving from the phone. They were burning with a deepening rage. When the phone rang, he snatched it from its cradle.

"Ah, you are eager, Spider," came the soft, taunting voice of the Chief. "It was good of you to wait for me tonight. I was afraid you would be too alert for mere bullets, but it was worth the chance."

Wentworth's lips bared his teeth in a smile that had no mirth. His words were as suave and polished as the Chief's. "Call on me sometime again, Snake. Any time. I'm anxious to see you."

"And Nita?" queried the Chief's mocking voice. "Would you care to see her?"

A spasm of anger distorted Wentworth's face. "Of course," he said making his voice calm with enormous effort. "You can, very easily," said the Chief. He waited for Wentworth to speak and when he didn't, talked on. "I understand that Kirkpatrick refused to take credit for the raid tonight and reported the Spider was chiefly responsible. He said that the Spider forced him to participate and that he attempted, in the end, to kill the Spider."

Wentworth swore mentally. Kirkpatrick was spoiling all his plans.

"This enhances your fame, Spider," said the Chief deliberately. "It gives you something to bargain with!"

"Bargain?" queried Wentworth as if puzzled.

"Yes, bargain," said the Chief. His voice grated... "Bargain for Nita's soul!"

Wentworth laughed lightly. "A bit melodramatic, aren't you, Snake? Soul is rather outworn as a synonym for life."

The Chief's laughter mocked his own. "I used the term advisedly," he said. "I do not plan to kill your Nita. I plan to make her an addict of the narcotics you so despise. When that has been accomplished—and I assure you it is quite easy to do—I believe she will be less exclusive, more apt to appreciate the casual friendship of men...."

"You dog!"

"Ah, Spider." The mocking laughter was a torment. "I'm afraid you are not quite so coldblooded as I had thought."

Wentworth clenched the phone like a weapon. Anger flamed within him like ignited gunpowder, died instantly to arctic rage that gripped his heart with pincers of torture.

He forced out laughter. "Sorry," he said. "Sorry to disappoint you, but once in a while, the utter filth and depravity of the criminal mind shocks me. No criminal, you know, is really intelligent."

"Ha!" exploded the Chief.

"He employs the most outworn weapons," Wentworth pressed on. "These weapons tend to undo him. But actually it is his lack of imagination, his inferior mental processes that trip him in the end."

Curses grated over the wire, checked abruptly. "The methods may be outworn, Spider," the Chief snapped, "but in your case I think they will be effective. This is my ultimatum. Either you phone to the newspapers your endorsement of the campaign we have humorously designated 'Making it smart to be dopey' and assist me in such ways as I demand, or your Nita becomes a dope fiend and—other equally unpleasant things."

Against his stubborn bidding, against the steel control of his mind, the dear face of Nita rose before Wentworth, her sweet warm mouth, her blue sympathetic gaze. He closed his eyes, squeezing them tightly to shut out that torture, but it persisted. He raised his lids. His breath was noisy in his open mouth.

"Well, Spider," asked the Chief. "Your answer is somewhat slow."

Wentworth's eyes were lambent flame. His voice issued between clenched teeth.

"The answer, Snake, is no. The answer is further that if you harm Nita, you shall die by the vilest torture the human mind can conceive. The venom of the Spider will be a titillation of exquisite joy beside it. Understand?"

SILENCE ANSWERED that, silence that bespoke the force of Wentworth's speech. When presently the Chief replied it was slowly.

"I do not temporize, nor swerve from the path I have set," he said heavily. "Tomorrow you will have a foretaste of what is in store for your Nita. Tomorrow night I will call again.

"Think well, Spider. I do not attempt to buy you off, but your brain would be useful in my organization. Do as I ask, and not only will Nita be restored to you, but you shall share, and share heavily in our profits. They are not small profits, Spider."

"The answer," said Wentworth deliberately, "will be the same."

"Stubborn youth!" The Chief sighed mockingly, his humor returning. "Tonight Nita shall pay for your stubbornness!"

The wire clicked dead. Wentworth automatically checked on the source of the call, but he knew in advance the report: "I am sorry, sir, the call came from a dial telephone. We cannot trace the call, sir."

It was ten o'clock that morning when the elevator boy brought Wentworth a picture that, carefully wrapped, had been left in the hall with the mail. Wentworth held the picture with hands like rock, but his heart trembled. It was a picture of Nita, but such a Nita as he had never seen before. He did not need the note of explanation to tell him that it had been taken while she was under the influence of the serpent's forcibly inflicted narcotics. It was plain to be seen in the distorted mouth, the hot half-closed eyes, the….

Wentworth shuddered in spite of himself. Savagely he ripped the picture to shreds, flung it across the room. He stood with feet braced, shoulders hunched. A madness of rage and hate glared from his eyes. His hands were gnarled fists at his sides and his chest panted, the breath hoarse in his throat.

Gradually he forced himself to calmness. The Bloody Serpent should pay for this and pay terribly. He threw back his head, his breath slowing. Meantime, it could be turned into a weapon against them. A smile cold as death touched his mouth. He strode to the phone and went through the long rigmarole of getting hold of "Dr. Skeen."

Wentworth allowed the Chief no time to taunt him. "You made an offer last night," he said. "I am ready to talk."

"Splendid," said the Chief softly. "I thought you would see the affair my way, after...."

"Cut that!" snapped Wentworth.

"I am not accustomed," the Chief bit back at him, "to—"

"Understand this right now," said Wentworth. "If I come into this thing, I come on equal terms with yourself. I will cooperate, but I'll take no orders from you or any one else."

Silence fell between them for the full space of a minute.

"For a man in your position," said the Chief finally, "you take a rather high tone, Spider."

"What I said goes," Wentworth told him flatly.

More silence, and finally the Chief's voice again. "Nothing is to be gained by such argument as this," he said. "We'd better get together and talk this over."

"An excellent idea," Wentworth agreed dryly, "but somewhat dangerous. You need expect no trust from me. I demand guarantees."

"Such as?"

"I will confer with you only, alone, and at a place I designate."

"Ha!" exploded the Chief, a snort of laughter. "Do you expect me to trust a cold-blooded murderer like the Spider?"

"Afraid?" taunted Wentworth.

"Merely cautious."

"You have a hostage," Wentworth pointed out. "I have no hold upon you whatsoever."

"An idea!" cried the Chief. "I will send Tess Goodleigh to you as a hostage, her life forfeit if we attack you!"

Wentworth smiled grimly, thinking of a girl dead with a knife in her back—they valued their women highly! But he agreed ultimately.

"All right, then," said the Chief, and exultation shadowed his voice. "At eight tonight, leave your apartment. Travel anyway you like, taxi, afoot, or in an armored car. A chauffeur wearing a green livery and driving a scarlet Lincoln will guide you, picking up your car inside of a few blocks. Before eight Tess will come to your apartment."

WENTWORTH, IN the interim before Tess Goodleigh arrived, insolent in burning red, hand on a silk-sheathed hip, sent Professor Brownlee to his Long Island estate to make certain preparations.

"Howdy, big boy," was Tess Goodleigh's greeting. She dropped into a velvet damask chair, looked about her appraisingly. "I could put up with this dump," she drawled. She crossed her legs and was not careful with her skirts.

Wentworth bowed to her. "Sorry I can't remain to entertain you. If you will be kind enough to await my return—"

The girl grimaced at him. "I'll be here, all right. I'm to commit Hara-kiri if anything happens to you, so take care of yourself, big boy, take care of yourself."

Wentworth retired into his dressing room and there had Ram Singh fasten beneath his arms a belt with a steel hook attached at the back and which, at need, could be pulled above his collar. Over this he donned the disguise of Tito Caliepi, the Spider.

This done, he made a furtive exit by the servant's door, drove his Lancia down Fifth Avenue. The scarlet Lincoln, with its chauffeur in green, appeared before Wentworth—trailed at a distance by Ram Singh—had driven a half dozen blocks. He followed the car southward, then east, crossing the Bowery and boring, through narrow, twisting streets, into the heart of the tenement-congested East Side.

As they pushed on, Wentworth saw two other cars close in on him and roll along at a fixed distance behind. The Lincoln ahead turned south into a street wide enough for only a single car, little more than a dark, wall-crowded alley. The scarlet limousine ahead slowed, the two behind closed in. Without seeming to be more than casually interested, Wentworth peered about and found men posted in windows, others crouched in doorways. He smiled thinly. A clever trap and powerful. The Bloody Serpent was taking no chances with the well-known slipperiness of the Spider!

Wentworth spurted the Lancia with its bulletproof windows and sides until the gleaming, stream-lined nose was within feet of the rear of the scarlet Lincoln. He whirled sharply to the sidewalk then, bumped over the curb, then out and crowded against the leading car. With a startled glance, his face white, the chauffeur in green swerved over the opposite curb, tried to dodge away. Wentworth jammed side by side with him until the Lincoln was forced to halt, its fenders brushing the brick wall of a tenement.

Men darted from doorways, shouting. The machines behind closed in. Wentworth opened the left door of his car and, gun in hand, stepped into the Lincoln beside the chauffeur. The two open doors formed a bullet-proof passageway for him. He pressed the automatic into the man's side, smiling pleasantly.

"The traffic was becoming a bit congested," he said. "Drive on."

The cars behind squawked furious horns, stopped by Wentworth's Lancia virtually broadside in the street. The Lincoln surged forward.

"Drive fast," said Wentworth "I'm afraid we'll be late for the conference."

The chauffeur jerked his eyes swiftly sidewise, felt gun steel prod his ribs and stepped on it. Six blocks further on, the pursuit lost in the tangle of the streets for the moment, the Lincoln halted before a dingy tenement.

"I'm afraid this street is muddy," Wentworth murmured. "Would you mind driving around to the back way?"

The chauffeur stared at the cobbled street, glanced at Wentworth's grimly smiling face and jerked the car forward. He circled the block and, at further orders, jerked the car over the curb and against a tenement door so that Wentworth, stepping from its bullet proof protection, was entirely shielded by the brick walls of the house itself. He walked into the blackness with a leveled gun, the cane tucked casually under his arm, went through the house, vaulted a fence with noiseless ease and entered the tenement before which they first had stopped.

UTTER SILENCE greeted him, yet the house did not have the feel of an empty building. The silence thickened. Wentworth sat down in a black corner, rested his gun on his knees and waited. Within minutes two cars slammed to a halt and men, cursing, strode heavily into the hall.

"The Chief's gonna be sore as hell," a man muttered. "Imagine the nerve of that guy, blocking the street and driving off with our own car!"

"Aw, dry up," another growled at him. "I'm trying to think up an excuse."

"It better be good," another thrust in.

The house received these men silently, too. They trooped upstairs and as they passed him in the darkness, Wentworth rose and joined in their noisy climb. The men paused in a black hallway, rapped on a door.

A calm "Come in" seemed to disconcert the men. They shuffled feet.

"Might as well go in and face it," one muttered firmly. "Go on, open the door."

There was more delay and the soft vole beyond the door called again before finally the knob was twisted and the men shuffled in to confront the Chief. He sat behind an unpainted wooden table, face muffled as always between hat brim and white muffler. A scarlet serpent ring glowed on his finger. Wentworth lingered in the darkness of the hall, peering in.

"Well?" the Chief demanded sharply.

No one spoke. The men looked shame-faced and shuffled their feet noisily.

The Chief leaned forward, "So he got away from you, did he?"

One of the men in front gestured. "Geez, Chief, that guy is like greased lightning. One minute we got him…."

The Chief nodded slowly. "And the next you haven't," he concluded.

"That's it," said the gangster. "That's it exactly."

The Chief stood slowly, hands hanging at his sides. There seemed no menace in his poise, yet the men shrank back fearfully.

"Where is he?" the Chief demanded.

Several men burst into voluble speech at once. They told how Wentworth had evaded them in the narrow street.

"And when we gets around the block," one concluded, "the Lincoln ain't nowhere and neither is the Spider."

"Get out of here!" the Chief thundered. "I don't know why I content myself with such miserable vermin for help. I'll get rid of every last one of you nuisances and… *Get out!*"

The men shambled out, trooped off downstairs. When the last had gone, Wentworth stepped up to the door and knocked.

"Get out!" the Chief's voice roared.

Wentworth knocked again. He heard the Chief's feet slap the floor as he pounded across to the door, jerked it open. Wentworth held his cane ready. He pressed it against the Chief's forehead.

"Sorry I'm a little late in getting here," he said politely. "I was delayed by a traffic jam. Let us go in and be seated."

The Chief's eyes narrowed to pinpoints on Wentworth's own, but his voice was soft. "So sorry my escort missed you," he said with equal courtesy. "I was just scolding the poor fellows. They feel awfully bad about it."

Wentworth nodded gravely. "So I should imagine." He pressed lightly with his cane, and the Chief stepped backward precipitately, dropped finally behind the table while Wentworth took a seat at its end where he could watch both the door and the Chief.

"Now then," said the Spider, "there were certain matters we wished to talk over." His cane lay on the table; his automatic was in his hand.

"Yes," agreed the Chief, leaning back calmly, "but certain of my associates must arrive first. I couldn't act without them and we would save time by delaying matters until they arrive."

WENTWORTH, HIS eyes alight, nodded. He drew his platinum and black cigarette case and offered it to the Chief, tucked one between his own lips and lighted both. He leaned back. Blue threads and billows of smoke rose between them, stretched out in thin layers across the room.

"I must compliment you on your thoroughness last night," said the Chief. "Wiping out twenty men practically single-handed is quite a feat even for the Spider."

Wentworth waved the hand that held the cigarette negligently, and the thread of blue smoke wove a pattern in the air.

"I have not your genius for organization," he said in turn.

"Such a venture as yours requires a vast amount of it, a great deal of training of executives. The matter of replacements alone is considerable. You lost Harrigan and O'Tooley in one night… now twenty men."

The Chief's eyes glinted. "Which is one of the reasons, my dear Spider, that I wish you to become one of us."

The voice was soft but there was venom behind it. For a man recently outwitted in a plot against his enemy's life, he seemed singularly well satisfied with himself. A buzzer sounded softly at a distance. A man whistled off key. The Chief rubbed his hands.

"My associates are arriving," he said with satisfaction. There was a gleam of triumph in his eyes. Wentworth picked up his cane and, resting his elbow on the table, poised the ferrule before the Chief's eyes.

"I hope for your sake," he said softly, "that it is your associates. If it should be another of your little traps, it would fare ill with you."

Tension grew slowly within Wentworth. Silence continued over the house like a shroud. The buzzer did not sound again, nor did he again hear the distant off-key whistle. Wentworth had risked his life, the success of all his plans against the Bloody Serpent, to invade this den of snakes tonight, and he didn't intend to have them miscarry through any slip-up. Better to kill the Chief and take his chances on getting away.

The door knob began to revolve silently. Wentworth, seeing it, smiled quietly. He slipped into place the terrifying celluloid fangs.

"They do not bother you, I know, my dear Snake," he told the Chief in an undertone, "but your men are more impressionable. The twisted figure of the Spider with his fangs and his poisoned cane are fearsome things...."

He broke off as the knob stopped its revolution and the door began to ease inward.

"Come in, come in," he called in the flat, mocking voice of the Spider. "The Chief and I are ready for you."

The door stopped, then flung wide and three men sprang into the room with leveled guns. They halted, weapons leveled, stared from the Chief, with the venom-tipped cane at his forehead, to the crouching Spider *with* his fanged smile.

"Are these your associates, my dear Snake?" asked Wentworth gently. "They look more like thugs. I am afraid that you have tricked me again."

"Shoot him," the Chief ordered calmly. "I am not afraid of this poison needle of his. Shoot, I tell you."

Wentworth jerked an eye-corner glance at the Chief, looked back to the three men.

"Move a step, or a finger," he ordered curtly, "and the Chief dies. That means an end of easy money for all of you." Why didn't Ram Singh signal? The success of all his plans depended on him. Was it possible that he had lost the trail, had failed to locate this gang's headquarters?

"Shoot!" the Chief repeated.

One of the men lifted his weapon tentatively. Wentworth's hand was forced. He must strike now.... He jabbed with his cane. The needle snapped instead of penetrating.

"Shoot!" the Chief cried again, reeling back before the thrust of the cane. "I told you he couldn't hurt me!"

WENTWORTH SPRANG toward the Chief. The cane whistled in the air, swinging in a horizontal arc, cracked behind the man's ear. Guns blazed behind him, missed in the first shouting excitement of his attack. Before they could steady, Wentworth had caught the Chief, sagging in unconsciousness, from behind and using him as a shield, leveled a revolver, the cane abandoned on the floor.

Somewhere in the distance a shrill, high whistle rang out piercingly, and Wentworth, smiling mockingly, backed toward the window.

"There will be orders for you later tonight," he told the three men with their leveled but impotent guns. "Hold yourself in readiness for them, and see that they are obeyed to the letter."

He reached the window, stepped backward out of it and paused for a moment, straddling the sill. He reached up behind his neck for a moment with his gun hand, but before the men could take advantage of it, before they could charge against him and rip his protective human shield aside, the gun was leveled again. He locked his arms about the heavy Chief and then, while the gangsters stared in amazement, he drifted backward into the darkness.

For an instant the lights of the room showed the pale, hanging face of their leader, the mocking gleam of the Spider's fangs behind him, moving swiftly backward into the night. Then the blackness closed about them and they were gone.

They stared at the window, converged on it in a swift rush,

peered out into the shadows. Not a sound, not a movement!...
But wait!

There was sound—sound that made them shudder and shrink
away from that open window in fright. It was the flat, mocking
laughter of the Spider!

CHAPTER 16
CELL OF MADNESS

WHAT SEEMED so mysterious to the gangsters left
behind had been a simple affair. Wentworth, reaching
up behind his neck, had simply attached the hook and harness
he had donned earlier in the night to a silken cord that Ram
Singh had strung for him—the whistle was the signal that all
was ready—and Wentworth and his prisoner had slid down the
cord into the dark hallway of the tenement back of that in
which the gang had set its trap.

As soon as Wentworth's feet struck the floor, he turned his
prisoner over to Ram Singh and darted ahead of him through
the hallway, spied from its darkness into the street beyond. As
he watched, flames leaped up in the car Ram Singh had used.
The gangsters had set it afire. By its light, the Spider made out
a dozen men waiting in the shadows with ready guns.

He hurried back to Ram Singh and, the two of them carrying their prisoner, they made their swift way upward through
hallways lit vaguely by sputtering gas jets. The roof scuttle was
off and the heavy, dust-thick air of the city's May night drifted
in through it. Wentworth, tossed by Ram Singh's ready hands,

The instant he was revealed in the dim
light, the chief threw up his automatic
and fired at Wentworth.

caught the scuttle's edge and muscled himself upward cautiously. Two cigarettes glowed against a chimney. There was a glint beside them that was a Thompson submachine gun.

"Hey, you two," Wentworth called gruffly. "Give me a hand, will you?"

The two started. Cigarettes snapped away and the glitter that was the machine gun leaped to their hands.

"Give me a lift, will you?" Wentworth repeated. "There's new orders from the Chief. That damned Spider…" he let his voice become indistinct.

One of the men hurried forward. As he neared, Wentworth swung himself upward, and springing to his feet, closed his fingers about the man's throat before he could cry a warning. Their shoes scuffed the gravel-spattered roof.

"What's the matter?" the other man called sharply.

"This guy's heavy as hell," Wentworth grunted out in hoarse imitation of his enemy's voice. "Can't seem to get him…."

The second guard hurried toward them and Wentworth, swinging to the jaw of his first antagonist, leaped upon the second with flailing fists before he could shout a warning. It was the work of moments then to haul up the Chief and Ram Singh, to bind and gag the two prisoners and make their way rapidly over roofs to the end of the block.

There, by means of skillfully thrown lengths of the weighted silk cord, Wentworth and Ram Singh bridged the street. Wentworth crossed it hand over hand, his palms padded with wrappings of cloth. He hauled the Chief across on the harness Wentworth had used previously with another length of cord tied about his waist, then Ram Singh crossed as had Wentworth. When they had gone another block, they had broken through the cordon of the gang and it was possible to descend to the street. Supporting their reviving prisoner between them they walked to a cab.

At Wentworth's Fifth Avenue apartment, entered openly now with disguise removed, he found Tess Goodleigh, still waiting. She showed no surprise at his entrance with his prisoner. Leaving Ram Singh to watch her, he took the Chief, bound hand and foot, into another room and flung him across the bed.

He flipped off the white muffler, and the hat, and the wiry long white hair was exposed, and his broad, sagging florid jaws. There was no doubt about it. This was Senator Bragg to a hair.

The Chief smiled calmly up at Wentworth. "Just what do you expect to accomplish by this?" he demanded. "If you harm me, it will be many a day before you see Nita. And when you do see her, you'll wish you hadn't."

Wentworth stared down at him unwinkingly, his gray-blue eyes cold.

"I have now a hostage of some value," he said. "I know that you would not hesitate to sacrifice Tess Goodleigh, if it would accomplish your ends. You proved that tonight. But with you in my power, I will have no more difficulty." He sat upon the side of the bed. "We have still a lot to talk over," he went on, "and now there is nothing to disturb us."

They talked for four hours. In the end, the Chief of the Bloody Serpent was convinced that, regardless of what fate he decreed for Nita Van Sloan, this cold-eyed man with the thin-lipped determined mouth, would push through to the end of his plans. If it cost Nita's life, the Spider might be a broken man in his heart, but the Chief and his mob would pay the penalty horribly. The Chief capitulated and agreed to a deal whereby Wentworth became his partner in the Bloody Serpent. The other conditions of the pact were that Wentworth's Long Island estate was immediately to become the headquarters of the gangs. Nita was to be taken to the estate, and she would serve as the Chief's hostage while he himself would be Wentworth's.

Wentworth seemed foolishly positive that he could keep the Chief under his thumb, only smiling slightly when this was commented upon. So confident was he that he agreed to take to the estate only his personal servant, Ram Singh, and to allow the Chief to surround the place with his gangsters, to permit them to build it into a stronghold that it would take an army to crack.

When these things had been agreed upon, the Chief set in motion the machinery which would call together all the leaders of the mobs throughout the country. They were already in the city, summoned to combat together the mounting strength of federal and police opposition, bolstered by the Spider's persistent harrying. When this had been done the two men, Ram Singh driving, Tess Goodleigh lounging between them with a cigarette dangling from her bitter red mouth, they drove to Wentworth's Long Island estate.

IT WAS the next afternoon before the hordes of gangdom began to arrive in force, carloads of shallow-eyed killers and ape-shouldered strong-arm men. And, riding in suave limousines, bullet proofed and convoyed, came the over-tailored, over-barbered overlords of the Underworld. With each new carload, the arrogance of the Chief mounted. About his neck on a cord dangled a silver whistle. If he blew that, Nita was to die, Nita whom Wentworth had not yet seen, whom he would not see, under the terms of their agreement, until after the conference of the gang leaders this night.

Wentworth carried no silver whistle, but Ram Singh, gun and knife at his belt, was ever at his back, and Wentworth himself was ever with the Chief. At the first overt move, the Chief was to die. When light fell finally, the estate was full to overflowing with the army of crime. The caretaker's lodge, the guest house, even the vast stables and garages, were crowded with the men. A ceaseless patrol of them wandered about the shrub-planted lawns.

Finally the conference hour was at hand. The library was lined with chairs, and at the broad flat desk sat Wentworth in the Spider habiliments which he had worn since his arrival at the estate. Beside him sat the Chief, his white hair hidden by a hat, a white muffler masking the lower half of his face.

When the door had been closed behind the last one of them, Wentworth rose behind the desk and waited, peering about the crowded room until all had fallen quiet. There were men of every race and nationality here, in chairs tilted back against the book-lined walls; standing beside the mantle where two seven-branched candle-sticks blazed with lighted wax tapers; sprawling at ease on the divan.

"I have asked the Chief," Wentworth said, "and he has agreed that each of you is to make a detailed report on his organization and what it does, its numbers and its split of the profits. Will you begin, please?" He nodded to a dark-visaged man at his left.

The Chief rose to his feet as the man started to talk, and silence fell again on the room.

"This is entirely superfluous," he said. He drew a revolver from his pocket and leveled it at Wentworth. "I will eliminate this troublesome gentleman, the Spider, and save a lot of talking."

Wentworth laughed good-naturedly. "Sorry to disappoint you, Chief," he said, "but I'm afraid I can't allow you to shoot me."

"No?" asked the Chief softly.

Wentworth shook his head, still smiling.

"And why not?"

Wentworth strolled across to the mantel piece. "Would you gentlemen mind moving?" he asked those grouped in front of it.

They glared at him, turned to the Chief. He shrugged his shoulders. "Let him play the fool a while if he likes," said the man behind the white muffler. "He can't do anything."

"Thank you," said Wentworth, bowing to the Chief. He stood before the mantel. "I'm going to show you now why you can't kill me, gentlemen," he said, as if apologetically, and, raising his hand, slowly pointed toward the central candle of the set of seven on his right. While a man might have counted three, nothing happened, then there was a smashing tinkle of glass from the windows, followed immediately by the smack of a powerful blow on the wall above the mantel.

Men's eyes darted from one spot to the other. In the window, there was a round hole from which cracks radiated. In the wall above the mantel was a circle of torn plaster. The candle at which Wentworth had pointed was out, its wick snapped off clean. Distantly, as the men stared open-mouthed, came the faint crack of a high-powered rifle.

WENTWORTH, STILL smiling faintly, lifted his right hand and pointed to the central candle of the other set of seven. Again the smash and smack of a speeding bullet, the distant faint crack of a rifle.

Wentworth stepped to one side so that he stood before the candles and placed his hand upon a French clock whose sides were plate glass. He twisted the clock about and showed them, fastened to its back, a bottle of brown liquid.

"My life insurance," said Wentworth casually.

"What do you mean?" demanded the Chief sharply.

"That," said Wentworth, nodding toward the bottle, "is nitroglycerin. All over the house at spots that my riflemen know, bottles like that are planted. If I give the signal, bullets will set off the nitro. Do I make myself plain?

A man darted toward the window, hand raised for the shade.

"I wouldn't do that," said Wentworth gently. "If that shade is drawn, or if I disappear from sight once, it is a signal for the riflemen to start shooting. I might point out also that if the lights go out, that also would be a signal, and the bullets still could find the bottle of nitro—since all of them have been varnished with luminous paint."

The Chief picked up the silver whistle that dangled about his neck, put it beneath his muffler. Between his teeth, it made an odd bulge in the white silk. His voice was distorted by it.

"Order all your riflemen here at once," he ordered grimly, "or I'll blow this whistle, and Nita will die."

Wentworth shook his head slowly. "She would die anyway," he said calmly, "if I submitted to you. I prefer it this way. Nitroglycerin will be about as near as possible to instantaneous death."

The opening of the door whirled every man toward it. Tess Goodleigh sauntered in, insolent as always. She looked at none of them but the Chief, her right hand resting lazily on her hip.

"Listen," she said, "how long is this damned pow-wow goin' to last? I'm getting damned fed up with just sitting around doing nothing."

"Get out of here," the Chief said shortly.

The girl's red mouth curved mockingly. "Uh-uh," she said. "I don't want to."

Every eye in the room was fixed on her, wavering from this impudent moll to the Chief. Wentworth dropped his hand beside him and touched what appeared to be the lever of a chimney draft regulator. A steel plate shoved out from the side of the window, began to slide across it. Another gray plate slid across the door. Once more glass tinkled from the window. The rifleman had shot out the lights!

Wentworth dashed the candle sticks to the floor, sprang aside as flame belched from the automatic in the Chief's hand. Men shouted out in fear, chairs crashed to the floor, feet trampled.

"Stop shooting!" A man's voice cried desperately. "You'll hit one of us!"

"The nitroglycerin!" Another screamed. Fists beat dully on the steel door.

"Let's have a light," said the Chief's calm voice. "He can't get out. Why he's locking the door and window I don't know."

A flashlight stabbed its white beam across the room. A pistol blazed and the light went out. Twice more that happened, and the Chief's fast shots accomplished nothing.

"Everybody stand still," the Chief ordered grimly. "I don't know what the purpose of all this is, but it's obvious by now that there isn't any nitroglycerin planted unless it's in that bottle on the mantel piece. Spider, surrender, or I blow the whistle and Nita dies."

Mocking laughter that seemed to come from everywhere, but nowhere definitely, answered him. "Go ahead and blow," said Wentworth. "They couldn't hear you through that steel if you used a steam whistle!"

Without warning, a man screamed hoarsely. "God!" he cried. "The Spider stung me!"

Once more the all pervading laughter mocked them.

"Remember how Whitey Maxwell died?" The Spider's voice asked softly. "After I stung him, his face began to swell and a pain like a knife ran through his brain…."

"Oho-hhhhh!" moaned the man he had stung. He screamed, "My head!"

Laughter again, flat, merciless, mocking.

"It takes twenty-four hours to die," said the Spider. "Twenty-four hours of torture in hell!"

Another man screamed, "I'm stung!" A third was inarticulate with fear and pain. Then in that black, close prison, men began to go mad. Guns belched flame in the darkness, books spilled from shelves, furniture crashed to the floor. Men shouted, shrieked, cursed. And now and then one screamed with the pain and fear of the Spider's sting, questing him out in the darkness, striking terror to his heart, tearing at his brain with claws of crazy fright.

WENTWORTH LAUGHED above that bedlam. The Chief shouted vainly to quiet the men.

"Quiet," Wentworth snapped suddenly. "Quiet if you would live!"

Even to those panic-ridden men, his words penetrated. Life was what they wanted, escape from this black-hole where death struck painfully and without warning in the dark, struck with the promise of long hours of fearful torture. Finally the bedlam died, died except for the moans of those who suffered, torn by the pain of the sting.

"There is a way to save yourselves," Wentworth said slowly, letting each word sink in. "Those who confess will be allowed to go to the prison I have built in the cellar and await police. Those who resist shall die of the Spider's sting. There are dictographs here, ready to record what you say. Just speak."

"I'll kill the first man that speaks!" The Chief's voice cut through the thick silence like a knife.

Wentworth sent once more his eerie laughter into the room. "But not as slowly as I will!"

And suddenly another man screamed. "God! *The sting of the Spider!*"

Voices babbled after that, mad frightened voices begging to be allowed to confess, anything to escape the madness of death by torture in the black, close prison of the room from which not even the sound of their voices could escape.

"One at a time," ordered Wentworth. "You in the corner by the door, talk first."

"I'm Gyp Loretti," he babbled out, "I'm in charge of—"

Flame from the Chief's pistol. A cry from the man who had tried to talk, a cry—then an answering spear of fire. Two more shots from the Chief. Silence from Gyp Loretti.

"Who's next?" asked the Chief brittlely. "Now listen, you fools! Every man strike a light of some kind, match or flashlight. We'll all rush Wentworth and kill him! He may get some of us, but if he gets confessions, most of us will go to the chair. Altogether, when I say the word."

"Light?" asked Wentworth gently. "Why, if light is all you want...."

Slowly a glow of rose began in the corners of the ceiling, spread like dawn thrusting aside the curtain of the night. A faint roseate illumination dropped over the room, revealed Wentworth standing before the fireplace with a stinging cane in both hands. The instant he was revealed, the Chief threw up his automatic and fired the full clip directly at Wentworth. The Spider did not even waver. He threw back his head and laughed.

"Haven't you learned yet that I'm invulnerable?" he asked gently.

More bullets pounded at him. Wentworth walked slowly toward the Chief, a cane poised. Six men were writhing in agony on the floor. Their cries and moans filled the room. "Your turn, Chief," said Wentworth, and he pointed the cane not at his forehead, but at his cheek.

The Chief staggered back, throwing up his arms.

"This is the last call," said Wentworth, his voice ringing sharply. "Confess now, or the light goes out again and you all will taste the sting of the Spider."

The Chief started to protest harshly. But already his men had begun to pour out their confessions; their names and identities; what part they had in the dope work; what their men did; who they were—all the details of the vast organization that the Chief had built up. Finally, it was finished. The last man had told his story.

Wentworth still held the cane level at the Chief's face.

"It is your turn," he said gently.

The Chief straightened, his eyes glinting. He took off his hat. "I will never confess," he said. "Senator Tarleton Bragg may die, but he'll never surrender." His white hair was like a knight's crest.

WENTWORTH THRUST the cane a little nearer the man's cheek. But instead of jabbing, he did a curious thing. When the cane was within an eighth of an inch of the Chief's unyielding face, he flipped the ferrule up sharply. There was a sound of metal rasping on metal, and the entire top of the Chief's head lifted!

It was fantastic in that weird, red light. The top of his head seemed to be tossed clear of the rest. That sprouting, wiry white hair lifted and spilled to the floor and revealed the smooth blond hair, the bulging, knotted forehead that Wentworth knew. The Chief, the man who had posed as Senator Tarleton Bragg, was none other than Claudius Mobo! His disguise had been a steel skull cap to hide that telltale forehead.

"Damn you!" Mobo shrieked, plunging toward Wentworth. He snatched at him, but inches from Wentworth's body his hands struck something that turned them aside.

"Glass!" screamed Mobo. "He's wrapped in bullet-proof glass! He's wearing a suit of the damned stuff over his body and head!"

Wentworth struck out with a cane and sent him reeling into the mantel piece. He leaned on it, panting heavily, staring about with wild eyes. The bottle of brown liquid, the bottle Wentworth had called nitroglycerin was at his elbow. With a cry, he snatched it up, raised it on high.

"You'll never live to boast of this, Spider," he shouted. "You'll die with—"

From the cowering ranks of the men against the far wall, a pistol spat. Once, twice, three times it spoke and at each crack Mobo's heavy body swayed and jerked. From behind a heavy chair across the room, Tess Goodleigh rose into sight. Her face was completely calm, her eyes steady. Coolly, she raised her pistol and fired twice more.

A strong shudder swept Mobo. The hand that grasped the

brown bottle became a rigid fist. Men raced to the door, pounded desperately on it. The clenched hand of Mobo became white. His head threw back, the bulging knotted forehead frowning as he fought to wrest one last moment from Death. His will seemed to hold him together. He tossed the bottle stiffly toward Tess. She cried out once. A great gulp of laughter snorted from Mobo, and he pitched forward, dead, to the floor.

The bottle struck the chair behind which Tess crouched, bounced and smashed upon the floor. There was the thin tinkle of breaking glass, but no explosion. Thick brownish fumes began to rise. The rose lights grew dim, faded slowly into blackness. Men screamed.

CHAPTER 17
THE SPIDER IS GENEROUS

"W2VI CALLING WRKA. Station W2VI calling WRKA. Hel-loo WRKA. W2VI calling WRKA. WRKA!"

Wentworth said it monotonously over and over as his black, silver-winged plane sped southward. And presently, rasping back into lets ear-phones, came the answer, "Hellooo W2VI. This is WRKA."

Wentworth laughed softly. "Hello, Kirkpatrick. I'll tell you now why I wanted you out on Long Island. If you'll go to my estate, you'll find the basement full of strong-arm men and gangsters. They yielded to the persuasion of machine guns behind steel armor. In my library are their leaders, and you'll find dictographs there with full confessions. You recall how those steel panels of the room operate? Well, the leaders are all unconscious. At the last minute, the leader, Claudius Mobo, threw what he thought was nitroglycerin at his conqueror but it was only narcotic gas."

"How did you do it?" Kirkpatrick's strong, alert voice demanded over the air.

"Some other time, Kirk. Professor Brownlee rigged it all up in advance and hid a bullet-proof glass case in the room for me," Wentworth told him. "There were two holes through which I put my arms and used the Spider's sting. They never thought to shoot at my arms"—he laughed softly—"they were too intent on killing me and bullets that strike the arms don't kill. Good luck to you Stanley, And hurry! When you bring in this batch of prisoners and the confessions, they'll make you governor at least."

"I won't take credit," Kirkpatrick said sharply.

Wentworth laughed. "Then you want to brand me as the Spider," he demanded. "Why do you think I staged all this at my estate? If you go to the city and say the Spider did this, they'll hang Richard Wentworth to a sour apple tree!"

Kirkpatrick's curses brought more laughter to Wentworth's lips. Red dawn was in the east. He turned in his seat and grinned at Nita, smiling back at him from the rear cockpit. She had on ear-phones and was listening in.

"Just one more thing before I sign off," said Wentworth. "Nita and I are flying to Florida for a much needed rest. You'll find a girl unconscious in the room there too. She's Tess Goodle-igh, a government agent.

"Yes, I know everything she did, including putting one of her colleagues on the spot. But she did her best to get help to him, and it was necessary to do that to establish herself fully with the gang. She thought for a while tonight that I was really the Spider, but I finally convinced her that she was wrong. The Spider, you know, never leaves a living witness." Wentworth laughed. "Even Hendricks, down in Washington, didn't know Tess was working on the case. She had high authority, Kirk, the highest. She's secretary to Senator Tarleton Bragg ordinarily."

"I've got men on the way over there, already," Kirkpatrick broke in. "How long will that gas last?"

"The room is closed. It'll last an hour or so yet," Wentworth told him. "And oh, yes, one last request. Tell Randall Towers that Grace Puystan is in Radder's Sanitarium being cured of the dope habit. When she comes out I think she'll be more friendly toward him."

Wentworth smiled back at Nita again, turned his face toward the sun.

"W2VI signing off," he said into the mouthpiece.

Nita's voice charmed his ears, coming through the headset phones of the plane.

"But Dick," she said, "how in the world is Kirk going to take credit for those men in the library when you stung them with your cane and tattooed your seal on their foreheads? When they die of the Spider venom, everyone will know."

"You think of everything, loveliness," Wentworth told her.

"The only thing is that I didn't use either tattoo or Spider venom—just a bit of wasp poison to make them think they were hurt so they'd confess. This is once the Spider can forego the credit for the conquest."

Kirkpatrick's cars bored the dawn wind to Wentworth's estate. The plane was a dot in the roseate sky of a new day....

POPULAR PUBLICATIONS
HERO PULPS

LOOK FOR MORE SOON!

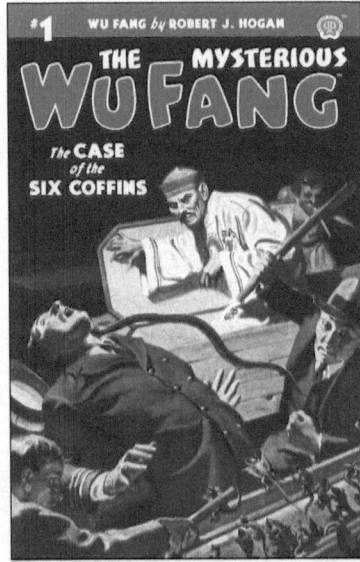

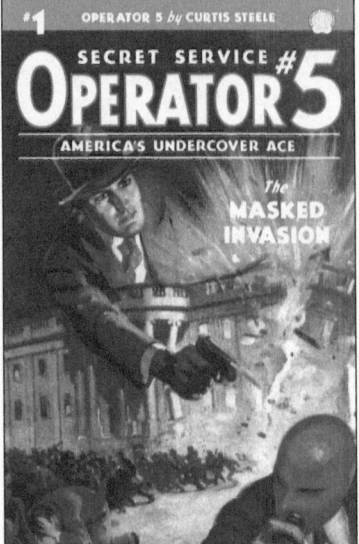